To: Pauline
Happy Xa

GOLD FEVER

Nancy Lou Deane

June 2019.

GOLD FEVER

❖

Nancy Lou Deane

authorHOUSE®

AuthorHouse™
1663 Liberty Drive
Bloomington, IN 47403
www.authorhouse.com
Phone: 1-800-839-8640

First published by AuthorHouse   07/08/2011

ISBN: 978-1-4567-8316-7 (sc)
ISBN: 978-1-4567-8317-4 (ebk)

LIbrary of Congress Number: 2011909169

Printed in the United States of America

DEDICATION

This story is written with fond memories of the happy years the author spent in Australia

GLOSSARY OF AUSTRALIAN TERMS

A bit crook	-	To feel ill.
A billy can	-	A lightweight can hung over a camp fire and used by stockmen, drovers and swagmen to make strong sweet tea.
Billabong	-	Backwater of a river.
Bush	-	Australia's uninhabited areas.
Bush bread	-	Dough made from grinding seeds into paste.
Bush tucker	-	Aboriginal food.
Corroboree	-	Ceremonial meeting acting out events from the Dreamtime.
Damper	-	Flat bread made from flour and water.
Dhakhan	-	Aborigine Spirit of the Rainbow and Waterholes.
Didgeridoo	-	Aboriginal musical instrument.
Dingo	-	Wild Australian dog.
Galah	-	A type of parrot.
Scrub	-	Dry tufts of grass.
Swagman	-	Walking traveller carrying his possessions in a bag on his back.
Tucker	-	Food.
Walkabout	-	To wander off into the bush for no reason.
Wallujabi	-	Aborigine Snake Spirit.

PREFACE

A group of Aboriginal elders met beside a campfire. A young man was brought into the clearing where they sat. Head held high, he listened carefully to their words, drank the snake's blood they offered. Gathered behind the elders, women swayed to the horn-like sounds of a didgeridoo. Chanting softly, they began to stamp their feet and beat skin drums with their bare hands.

The young man drifted back—to the time when the world had begun.

From outside his body he saw his shape change. 'Come.' A deep voice called. In his Dreamtime he followed the voice out onto the scrub plain along a ridge until he came to a waterhole where he drank, filling his body until it swelled up. Gradually he stepped into the water. His man's form took that of a snake and he wriggled through the water enjoying its silky feel on his skin. Then the voice spoke to him again. 'Dhakhan, you now rainbow snake, protector of people; punisher of our law breakers. Go to your people and give them wise words.'

In a trance, Dhakhan made his way back to camp where the elders received him, covering his body with blankets. The women disappeared back to their families, but the elders remained watching over the young man.

———

CHAPTER ONE

DARWIN, 1937

Lightning slashed through the sky.
Thunder clapped.
Rain drummed.
The cyclone hit.

Terrified, Stella Whitney shrank under the bedclothes, covered her ears, tried to shut out the noise. But the voice in her head kept willing her to have a look, to find out what was going on outside. Finally, unable to resist the voice, she flung the bedclothes to one side and stumbled on bare feet across the wooden floor to the window. The wind screeched around the house, throbbed in her ears. Pulling back the flimsy net curtain, she rubbed a hole in the steamed up window and squinted into the unnatural light. Through the rain she could just make out the drainpipe on the corner of the house overflowing onto the wooden hut her brother Billy had built for her, flooding the small area of grass around it. It was then she heard it—coming from further down the street—a roaring sound that got louder as it got closer. Not knowing what to expect, she clutched the corner of the curtain. Suddenly a huge sheet of water washed over the top of the wooden fence that divided them from the McDowell's next door. Sweeping everything with it, the wave charged on, filling the long drainage channel in front of the house, making it impossible to see where the grass finished and the drainage system began.

'Ma, where are you?' she sobbed into the curtain. 'You promised you wouldn't be long.' Rubbing the tears from her tired eyes, she glanced at the wooden clock on the wall. It was almost ten thirty. Flickers of fear stirred in her stomach. And where was Billy? He should have been home too. Something was wrong, she just knew it. When a mist began to gather over the sheet of water hiding everything from view, she turned from the window and crept back into bed. Afraid of the shadows that clung to the corners of the room, she pulled the sheet over her head. Hot again, she tossed the sheet onto the floor. Focusing her eyes on a spider on the ceiling playing with a fly caught in its web, she lay rigid, aware only of the wind shrieking and the rain drumming on the roof.

Chapter Two

Under a low light at the back of a bar in a hotel in Darwin, three men glanced warily at each other. Hands sweating, shoulders hunched, their faces gave nothing away.

Caught in a gambling fever, Billy clutched his cards to his chest. 'Mine, I think,' he said, fingers itching to touch the pile of neatly stacked chips. Slowly he placed his cards face up on the table, and without waiting for an answer, reached forward to gather his winnings.

'Not so fast Billy m' lad,' Zach, the oldest of the three, drawled. 'I've got four sevens.'

The atmosphere in the room tightened.

Zach slipped one hand under the table, sliding his long fingers down his leg until they touched the sheathed knife hidden in his boot. Very slowly and deliberately he laid his cards alongside Billy's.

Billy stared at Zach's cards. 'B . . . but,' he gasped.

'What . . . Billy? You thinkin' I cheated?'

'Well, I . . .' Billy stopped. Nervous, he stared at the cards, then up into Zach's hard eyes and realised, for the first time, just how dangerous the man was. For a moment his nerve failed, but then he remembered his ma and his sister Stella waiting at home and his courage returned. Grasping the neck of the whiskey bottle with a shaking hand, he took a long swig and staggered to his feet. Looking around the room at the faces of the men he thought were his friends, he shouted, 'I had the winning cards.'

'But you didn't Billy. You had two aces and two kings and I had four sevens—that means my cards were better than yours,' Zach said quietly, speaking through lips drawn into a thin line. 'You just thought you had a winning hand.' Deliberately he picked up all the cards and shuffled them. Eyes narrowed, he looked at Billy and said, 'You're nearly eighteen aren't you?' Billy nodded. 'Well then, be a man an' show us you've got some guts. All this,' he said, poking a finger in the direction of the money and stack of chips, 'against that bit o' paper of yours. You know the one I mean—the one with the gold strike you're always talkin' about.'

Billy stared first at Zach then Ned.

Unmoving, they stared back.

'C'mon Billy,' Ned urged. 'If you think your luck's running, there's a nice amount o' money there,' he said, pointing at the table. 'Real money, not just a bit o' paper. C'mon lad, just one more round.'

Billy glanced at the table. With that amount of money, he'd be able to buy his ma and Stella a new dress each and there'd still be plenty left over for food. Beads of sweat broke out on his forehead. The gambling fever had him in its claws. Fingers tingling, head bursting, he found himself saying, 'All right then, just the one round.' Slumping in the chair, he pulled a piece of paper from his money belt and placed it on the table.

Sensing the tense atmosphere, a group of men drinking at the bar moved as one to gather around the players, watching each card as it was dealt.

Slowly Billy turned up the corner of each card—his heart lurched—he felt sick. He couldn't possibly win with a hand like that. Shaking his head to clear his mind, he tried to work out what to do. Through the fog of whiskey fumes, he knew, if he valued his life, he would have to get out—and quickly. Before anybody realised what he was doing, he swung his arm against the whiskey bottle, knocking it over. As if in slow motion, the golden liquid streamed over the money and the chips.

'Now look what you've done, Billy,' Ned shouted, jumping to his feet. Dragging a dirty handkerchief from his pocket, he dabbed at the sodden bank notes.

Furious, Zach leaned forward, grabbed the bottle then turned to help Ned.

Immediately Billy saw his opportunity. He snatched the strike note from the pile of chips and rushed out of the bar into the stormy night.

Zach came to his senses first. 'Blow me if he hasn't taken the strike note. Never thought Billy had it in 'im,' he muttered. Still shaking his head in disbelief, he shouted, 'C'mon boys—down to Billy's place. We've gotta get that strike note back tonight. By mornin' the boy will have scarpered.' Ramming his bushman's hat on his head, he marched towards the door. As he opened it, the wind snatched at his clothes, caught at his breath. 'Wow, we're in for a rough'n this time,' he wheezed and tightening the sliding knot of the leather chin strap on his hat, he pulled the rim down over his eyes and headed into the storm.

CHAPTER THREE

The front door slammed. Ma at last! A sigh of relief escaped Stella's lips, but a moment later she heard her brother's voice cursing the weather. Wrapping her thin arms around her body, she listened to his unsteady footsteps.

Although 13, Stella was very thin and her tanned legs stuck out like sticks from under the sheet. Nervous, her long slender fingers pulled at the mass of blonde hair that framed her gold-flecked light brown eyes. She liked to wear her hair loose and although the local women gossiped about her, she didn't care. She liked to be outdoors, to play on the nature strip in front of the house. However, she was grown up enough to know she'd be the one who would have to make black coffee for her brother the next morning, to help him shake off the dark cloud that hung over his head.

Heavy hearted, she listened to her brother stumbling on the stairs. Although the rain had lowered the temperature a few degrees, the air was still stifling. 'A good storm will be the only thing that'll clear the air,' her mother had said as they ate the last morsels of bread and cheese she'd hidden away for their supper. 'There was a weather warning on the radio this morning, but they didn't say any more than that. I guess we'll find out soon enough if it's going to hit us,' she said, her tone suggesting she couldn't do anything about it anyway. Weary, she wiped the perspiration from her forehead. 'It sure is hot,' she muttered. 'I bet your Aunt Edna's having trouble with those kids of hers—always trouble in this weather they are,' she said, flapping the air with the corner of her apron. 'I think I'll go round to your Aunt Edna's, see if she's all right. Billy'll be back soon so you'll be OK. You can finish clearing the table and do the washing up. Oh, and don't forget Stella luv, if the storm's bad, hide under the table. It's good and solid,' she laughed, slapping her hand hard on the table top to prove her point. Then grabbing her old felt hat, she disappeared out the back door.

But that was hours ago. Overwhelmed by the shrieking wind and the pounding rain, Stella curled her arms around her bent knees and waited until she heard her brother's feet on the landing. Then, swinging her legs off the bed, padded over to the closed door. 'Ma's not here, Billy,' she called out. 'She went over to Aunt Edna's and hasn't come back yet,' she shouted, trying to make herself heard over the roar of the wind.

There was no reply.

Suddenly, the bedroom door crashed inwards, almost knocking her off her feet.

Thunder rumbled in the distance, lightning flooded the room.

Her brother's flushed face stared back at her. For a brief moment he hovered in the doorway then staggered into the room. 'Stella love,' he wheedled. 'I'm in a bit o' trouble.'

'What you done this time Billy?' she asked, smelling whiskey on his breath.

'I ain't done nothing Stella luv, well not really bad as you'd say, but I got no money to pay me debts.'

'Gambling debts, I suppose you mean,' she said wearily. 'What happened to your wages? Didn't you get paid today?'

'Yes, Stel,—but I thought if I could win a bit—it might make life easier for you an' ma. I was thinkin' of yer, honest I was . . .' He stopped as a banging on the front door shook the thin fibreboard house. 'Crikey Stel, they've come to get me. Quick, take this and get over to your Aunt Edna's,' he said and snatching off his hat, pulled out his pa's strike note from inside the sweatband. 'Give this to ma. She'll know what to do. I'll talk to them while you slip out the back. Hurry now. They'll have the door down in a minute.'

Unquestioning, Stella grabbed the piece of paper. 'OK Billy. Will you come over to Aunt Edna's?'

'Soon as I can. Now, off you go before they break the door down.' Another thunderous bang echoed up from below. 'Now git—before they get you as well,' he said over his shoulder as he headed down the stairs.

Stella pulled on her clothes, shoved the bit of paper into the pocket of her worn cotton dress and stepped quietly onto the stairs. Not waiting to see what happened, she grabbed a raincoat, fled down the path to the back lane, crossed the soaked grassy area they called the nature strip and headed in the direction of her Aunt Edna's house.

CHAPTER FOUR

Inside the house, from behind the curtain, Billy watched the group of men hammering at the door. He'd have to hide, but where? His eyes fell on the table. The cloth that covered it fell almost to the floor. Another blow and the door split in two. In an instant Billy was under the table. Dragging the tablecloth back into place, he folded his arms around his knees and waited.

'OK boys, give the place a good going over. We gotta find that strike note.' Zach's gravelly voice filled the room. 'And you never know, Billy's ma might 'ave some gold stashed away as well.'

Terrified, Billy listened to the men pulling things from the cupboards, flinging them on the floor. He knew Zach would be very thorough. He still hadn't forgiven ol' man Tom for giving the strike note to his father. Two years had gone by since his pa's last visit, but he remembered it as clearly as if it were yesterday. They'd been sitting in the shade of the ghost gum at the bottom of the garden when his pa had told him about ol' man Tom; how he'd washed and cleaned him during the last week of his life, bathing his hot dry skin with cool water and fanning his face with a palm leaf to keep the flies out of his mouth and nostrils. 'Ol' man Tom didn't 'ave any family Billy—that's why he gave me the strike note. He knew I'd go out there and find the gold,' he'd added quietly.

Two days later his pa had gone, but the sun scorched land had won in the end. Alone, in the desert, his pa had died of thirst. It was cattlemen who had found his body and notified the Rangers. He didn't have much

in the way of belongings and it was ma who'd given his hat to Billy. He
was the one who'd found the strike note hidden in the sweatband. He'd
read his pa's words so many times he knew them off by heart. *'Beware
the cave. It takes the lives of all those who go into it . . .'* he'd written,
but what did the words mean?

Under the table, Billy's thoughts were interrupted. The tablecloth
was jerked to one side and Zach's straggly bearded face appeared.

'Well, an' look who's here—hiding like a common thief,' Zach
sneered, bending almost double to get down to where Billy was hiding.
'It's Billy, the boy who stole my strike note. Ned,' he called to the tiny
man standing behind him. 'You're smaller than me—get him out from
under there—an' search 'im.'

Without warning, Ned's strong wiry arms grabbed Billy by the
collar, pulled him from under the table and shoved him into the nearest
chair. With his free hand he ripped the shirt from Billy's back. Billy
tried to cover his money belt, but Zach's sharp eyes had already spotted
it. 'And what have we got here?' he asked and with one swift movement,
slashed Billy's web belt in two. 'Thought you said you'd got no money
Billy?' he sneered. 'And the strike note? It's not 'ere, Billy. So where
is it?'

'I lost it Zach,' Billy mumbled and, seeing Zach's mouth twist in a
cruel smile, he knew he had to shield Stella. 'The wind caught at it as
I run home,' he lied.

Fortunately, just at that moment, the wind died away.

In the silence that followed, Ned wailed, 'Tis the eye o' the storm.
We gotta get out of 'ere afore the worst of it arrives. We'll not be able
to stand against the wind then. Leave 'im 'ere, Zach. He won't go far
in this weather,' he added, jerking his head in the direction of the storm

outside. 'If he does . . . well . . .' He left the sentence unfinished. 'I'm off before it's too late,' he said, heading towards the door.

Zach glared at him. 'Oh no you don't Ned. We'll be safer in here than outside and we need to keep an eye on young Billy—decide what to do with 'im.' He drawled the words softly, but his voice was menacing, dangerous. To the others in a louder voice, he said, 'We're staying here for the night boys. Tie him up,' he said nodding in Billy's direction. 'Then make yourselves at home.' Pulling up a chair, he straddled it. 'So, what *are* we goin' to do with you Billy lad?'

CHAPTER FIVE

Lightning streaked through the sleeting rain.
Gum trees creaked and groaned in the frenzied wind.
Palm trees doubled.

Shoes squelching, Stella sloshed over the sodden nature strip and across the empty stretch of ground where the boys played cricket. When at last she felt hard ground beneath her feet she knew she was on the path that led to the old wooden bridge over the river that separated the Old and New Settlements. At the bridge, she paused to get her breath. Clinging to the rickety handrail, she stared at the swirling water below. Normally so quiet and tranquil, angry waves now beat against the river bank, breaking down the wet and sodden earth. Nervous, aware the bridge might collapse at any moment, she hurried across, each plank squeaking and groaning with every step. On the other side, she stumbled to the bottom of East Street and turned the corner into Miller Street where her aunt lived. Expecting to see the familiar pink and white fibreboard houses standing neatly in rows, she pulled up with a start. There was nothing there. Through flashes of lightning she stood and stared. Where were the smartly painted houses? Sheets of corrugated iron that had once been roofs of orderly houses lay scattered across the street. Broken walls stuck out of the ground like rotten teeth and upturned carts lay on their sides.

Confused, Stella stared at the scene of devastation, took in the baby clothes strewn across the road.

What had happened?

Where was everybody?

Suddenly the wind dropped, the rain eased.

She turned a full circle, seeking anything that moved, but everywhere was still and silent.

Time stood still.

Horrified, she could only stare at the wreckage around her. As suddenly as it had dropped, the storm started again, but this time it was worse, much worse. It snatched at anything and everything it could find, whisking it into the air, throwing it down again. Determined not to give in to fear, Stella crouched on the ground, put her head between her knees. Like an angry animal about to strike, the wind threw her to the ground, grabbed at her clothes. And the rain lashed down. Wet hair plastering her head and face, skirt clinging to her legs, she crawled away.

CHAPTER SIX

'Ma, where are you?' Stella cried. As she struggled to get back to the bridge, she tried to think clearly. If Aunt Edna's house wasn't there, perhaps her mother had returned home, taking Aunt Edna and her children with her. In the dense rain she could easily have missed them. But her mind continued to swirl with unanswered questions. Unable to find any answers, she decided to go home, hoping that Billy had got rid of his nasty friends and her mother would be there waiting for her. Without knowing it, tears trickled down her face, mingled with the rain. Bewildered, she struggled on hands and knees through the swirling mud. Clinging to anything that was left standing, she forced her way through the storm. When eventually she got to the narrow wooden bridge, she stared at the muddy red water swirling angrily below. Red from the soil that had swept into it, the sparkling stream was now a raging flood. Grasping the flimsy handrail, she stepped onto the bridge, took a few steps, but her weight caused the water to push up between the planks of wood and slosh over her feet. Fear, swift and sudden, made her freeze—she couldn't move. But she had to do something. 'Get off the bridge Stella Whitney before the cyclone gets you,' she shouted into the rain. As if in answer to her cry, her feet began to move. Dragging one foot in front of the other, she took a few steps forward. She'd just reached the centre when there was a loud crack. In slow motion the bridge crumbled and a spout of red water surged upwards. Clinging to the bridge's wooden rail she took another step. Then, without warning, the bridge split in two and she tumbled headlong into the churning water.

CHAPTER SEVEN

The river closed over Stella's head. In desperation, she flapped her arms and kicked her feet. The surging torrent sucked her down. She held her breath until her lungs felt as though they were about to burst. The sound of gurgling water pounded in her ears, a drumming filled her head. Light headed, she knew she must be drowning, but she didn't care. She closed her eyes and let the river surround her.

Suddenly, she was shooting into the air. Sky and earth blurred. Up, up, she went. Strong arms around her waist guided her until she landed with a thump in a forked branch of a gum tree. After she'd got her breath back, she looked down. The gum tree seemed to be growing in the middle of the whirling river only a few yards from where the bridge had once stood. She was wondering what she should do, when she heard a voice calling.

'Missie, missie, give hand.'

She looked up.

There, a few feet above her head, an Aboriginal boy was sitting on a branch, dangling his brown legs in the air.

'Missie, take,' he said, holding out his spear, smiling down at her.

Stella knew Aborigines had lived in Australia for thousands of years and many of them now lived in the towns, but the white whirls and circles that covered this boy's face and ebony body scared her. 'Who are you? And why are you here?' she asked.

'Me, Dhakhan,' the boy replied, showing white even teeth. 'Dhakhan is Spirit of Rainbow—make you safe. Come,' he said holding out his spear again. 'Don't be afraid. Dhakhan, help you,' he said, reading the fear in her eyes.

Not knowing what else to do, Stella leaned forward and wrapped her fingers around the end of the spear. Immediately she jerked upwards, out of the tree, into the sky. All of a sudden they changed direction and they were diving towards the river, and the boy, sitting crossed-legged around the spear, guided it over the water. As they sped along he changed shape—his legs disappeared—became a fish's tail. Astonished, she could only watch as he guided the spear with his tail fin, creating a tunnel through the raging water. She had no idea how far they went—or how long they took. Spellbound, she held on to the spear and stared at the fish tail in front of her as they travelled from one river to another. Then, without warning, the dark brown body in front of her changed again. The boy's arms became wings and they shot into the air. Leaving the river behind, they flew along at such a speed that Stella could hardly breathe. It seemed ages, but it was probably only a few minutes, before Dhakhan glided down to earth like an aeroplane, landing on a long strip of sand beside a water hole in the middle of the desert. Dazed, Stella looked around. Why had Dhakhan brought her here?

CHAPTER EIGHT

At dawn, two days before the cyclone hit, a Chinese family left the safety of the shanty town in Darwin and headed south. Two donkeys pulled their covered cart first over the rough desert ground and sharp boulders then through tough soured grass.

At 15, Ah Fong was very agile and fit. Every day he practised the South China Martial Art, kung fu, keeping his body fit and his mind sharp. One morning just as dawn was touching the sky and he was about to start his daily kung fu exercises, Ah Fong saw a group of young Aboriginal men gathering around the waterhole near where he and his father Wang had made camp the night before. He was not afraid of the Aborigines, but he knew if he annoyed them they could easily kill him with their spears, so he hid behind a rock and waited for them to finish drinking. In the distance, a wild dog yapped. Suddenly one of the Aborigines turned and stared in Ah Fong's direction. Terrified Ah Fong waited, but after a while the young man lost interest and joined the other Aborigines who were walking towards the dying campfire where Wang and Ah Fong's mother Hua, were sleeping. Ah Fong tensed. He was about to make a noise, to draw their attention away, when the Leader of the group put up his hand and pointed his spear at a line of kangaroos on the horizon. Using sign language, they talked to each other, then, eager for sport, they jogged off in the direction of the kangaroos. When they had gone, Ah Fong breathed a sigh of relief. In future he would have to be more alert.

Wang shook his head and looked thoughtful when Ah Fong told him what had happened. 'You good lookout Ah Fong. But now, we travel through night. With stars to show us the way, we will make good time and not get caught by Aborigine,' he said.

Ah Fong nodded in agreement.

And so they travelled on journeying across dry sandy soil, then through long grass. Ah Fong found it difficult to guide the cart through the long grass and was relieved when it came to an end and they were slipping and sliding along dry earth. Following a rutted dry track they picked their way between huge boulders and mounds as tall as giraffes. He had wanted to follow the river so the donkeys would always have plenty to drink and his mother could wash in the cool water, but his father Wang thought differently. 'Stars bring us safely to Australia Ah Fong,' he said, 'and we will follow them till we get to place called Tennant Creek.'

Ah Fong bowed his head. His father had spoken and he must do as he wished.

CHAPTER NINE

Billy's chin drooped; his head fell onto his chest.

'Oh no you don't Billy lad, not till you tell us what you done with the strike note.'

Billy stared at the flint grey eyes that bored into him like pieces of steel. 'Now, where is it?' Zach demanded.

'I told you Zach. I lost it on my way back 'ere. The wind took it out o' my hand.'

'Billy lad, it's me Zach you're talking to, not some witless buddie o' yours. Now, for the last time, where's the strike note?' he growled. 'Tell me an' you can go to sleep.'

Billy concentrated on the shaft of early morning sunlight shining through the tiny window above the sink at the back of the kitchen. Ma would know how to get rid of Zach. Playing for time, he said, 'Ma and Stella'll be back soon and you know my ma, Zach, she won't stand no nonsense, she'll call the police.'

'Billy, it's four in the morning. She won't be home yet and you knows it. Now tell me where the strike note is 'afore I lose my temper. This storm's making me quite jittery. So, for the last time—where's the strike note?'

'I ain't got it Zach, honest. M . . . maybe I could draw the map for you. Would that do?' Billy suggested hopefully.

Zach put his hands in his trousers and gave a deep throaty laugh. 'How do I know you ain't cheating me Billy, Like yer pa? You're a chip off the ol' block yer know—easy with words. So, why should I believe yer?'

'Because I'm the only one who can take you to the place where the strike is,' Billy insisted, becoming aware it was possible he might be able to out-think Zach.

'Well that's better, Billy lad. But why are you so suddenly agreeable?' he asked. 'You still trying to cheat me—like father, like son eh?'

'No Zach, honest, I ain't. I ain't got the strike note, but I know it like the back of my hand.'

'Well Ned—what d'you say? You think he could take us there?' Zach asked, looking across the room to where Ned was busy pulling open cupboards, looking for something to eat.

A loud knocking at the door interrupted them.

Everyone in the room froze.

Zach tweaked the curtains, looked down the street. 'It's the police,' he said. 'What are they doing here Billy?'

'I don't know,' Billy said, yawning loudly.

There was another loud knock, followed by hammering.

'Quick, out the back lads, afore they find us,' Zach snarled and, hauling Billy to his feet, dragged him through the back door just as four lean policemen stepped through the broken front door, into the house.

CHAPTER TEN

Billy woke to a soft breeze on his face, the creaking of wheels and a movement under his body. Holding his throbbing head he waited, expecting to see Stella appearing with a mug of hot coffee. When she didn't, he called out—'Stella, luv, 'urry up with that coffee.' Still nothing.

'Stel?' he called softly this time. He was about to call again when Zach's face appeared in front of him. 'Zach? What're you doing here and where's Stella?' Billy stuttered, peering into the spot where the sun a few moments before had been dazzling him.

'Stella's gone Billy and so 'as your ma. Don' you remember?'

Billy shook his head. 'What do you mean gone? I remember . . .' he paused . . . 'A storm, there was a storm, but that's all I remember. Was it bad Zach?'

'Yeah Billy, it was very bad. You sure you don't remember nothin?' he questioned, staring down into Billy's bewildered face.

Billy shook his head. 'No I don't. So, tell me—what happened?'

'Your ma and sister both died Billy. The cyclone got 'em—it flattened your Aunt Edna's house killing everybody in it. Your ma was struck on the 'ead by a bit of corrugated roofing—we buried her in the cemetery a week ago—couldn't bury your sister though, they never found her body. They reckoned she must've been swept away in the floods. Drowned, the law said. An' you Billy, you've been sick with a fever ever since. But we looked after you, didn't we Ned?' he wheedled, glancing sideways at Ned who had joined him.

'Ma *and* Stella?' Billy's lips trembled.

'Afraid so,' Ned said, briefly touching Billy's shoulder. 'For now Zach, I think we'd better leave 'im to his sorrows. We can talk to him later,' he said, stepping back through the open flap. Zach gave Billy a long searching look then followed Ned outside.

Alone, inside the wagon, Billy tried to piece together what had happened. He remembered Zach and his friends breaking into the house, stripping him and pouring whiskey down his throat. After that—nothing! Now he was being told his ma and Stella had been killed in the cyclone. Overwhelmed by sadness, knowing he was to blame for his sister's death, his eyes filled with tears. He'd told Stella to go to Aunt Edna's, but he'd thought it was the best thing to do—to keep her away from Zach and Ned. Suddenly, a piece of the jig-saw slipped into place—he'd given Stella his father's strike note—the bit of paper Zach and Ned desperately wanted. And now he was in a wagon—going somewhere—but where? He could only guess Zach and Ned were after his pa's gold strike. He held his aching head. The only thing he was sure about was that he was in a wagon with two people he didn't trust. Grief-stricken, he laid his head back on the bunk and wept.

CHAPTER ELEVEN

The blinding sun beat down on the hot earth. Through the shimmering heat Stella could see a number of bark shelters in the shade of a giant rock. In the middle of the camp a group of young Aboriginal girls sat crossed legged around the fire, sliding beads onto a string. Suddenly, they jumped to their feet and started to dance, stamping their feet inside a circle of stones. Bare, apart from a leather waistband that hung almost to their knees, they laughed and danced in the afternoon sunlight. Stella, whose wet dress still clung to her body, felt strangely over dressed.

After a while, the girls left the fire and began to dance towards her. 'Come. Come with us,' they called, holding out their hands. Not sure what she should do, Stella hung back.

'My name's Rohanna,' the tallest girl said, walking towards her, taking her hand. 'Come, elders say I look after you.' She smiled, showing white even teeth and a pink tongue that lightened her stern appearance.

'I am Stella,' Stella replied, smiling uneasily. 'Is this your tribe?'

Rohanna nodded. 'Stars tell Elders you coming,' she said.

Elders—they ruled the tribes—Stella knew that much. Rohanna seemed a nice person, so she let her lead her to the camp fire. Giggling and whispering, the others followed.

Rohanna sat on a mat and patted a place beside her. 'Sit, eat,' she said, pointing at the heaps of nuts and berries that had been laid out.

Stella stared at Rohanna then at the nuts and berries. It was a long time since she'd had anything to eat and the sight of the food made her stomach rumble noisily. Leaning forwards, she took a large handful of nuts, followed by some berries. When she had finished eating, the girls took her down to a billabong to drink. The sun was hot and Stella was tired so she settled down in the shade of a rock and slept.

Later, when the sun was going down, Rohanna took her into the bush and showed her where to find fruit, flowers and wild honey. When Rohanna found a witchety grub and popped into her mouth, Stella shuddered and turned away, pretending to look for berries.

Rohanna laughed. 'Witchety, good grub', she said eagerly digging her stick into the red gum tree to find more.

Stella liked Rohanna. She had made her welcome and already she was beginning to look on her as a friend. She'd never had a close girlfriend before. She'd had a few friends in school, but they never saw each other outside school. She never knew why, but the girls' parents didn't seem to like her. So Stella had gone home, helped her mother and looked after Billy when he'd been drinking. With Rohanna things were different. They liked doing the same things and laughed at the same things. Rohanna made a digging stick for her, showed her how to throw a boomerang, how to collect honey ants and how to make Aboriginal bread from the spinifex and wattle seeds they collected. Laughing together they ground the seeds, mixed in water to make a dough then cooked the bread in the hot ashes

One day Rohanna said, 'Tonight, we have Corroboree.'

'Corroboree, what's that?'

'Corroboree is special meeting for Dreamtime,' she said. 'Tonight the Elders will welcome you to our Tribe. Elders say, you have yellow hair like sun, you bring luck to tribe,' she said.

That evening, when the Elders had had enough of the emu and wild turkey the men had caught and the women and children had had their share, Rohanna took Stella's hand and led her forward. 'Now it time for corroboree,' she whispered. First a single man holding what looked like a hollow pole sat down beside the camp fire. 'That's a didgeridoo, he's holding' Rohanna explained. The Elders, painted in white swirls and dots, sat cross legged in the middle of the camp. The others, their painted bodies ghostlike in the firelight, stamped their feet to the didgeridoo's horn-like sounds.

Suddenly another group of men holding shields and wearing painted masks, grabbed Stella by the arms and drew her into the centre, circling around her, getting closer and closer.

Stella flinched when they shook their painted sticks at her, but she carried on smiling. 'Wh . . . why are they shaking their sticks at me?' she asked.

Rohanna laughed. 'Stella not be frightened. They do welcome dance for you,' she said.

Suddenly a fierce looking warrior with a feathered headdress jumped into the ring and pointed his spear first at Stella's heart then at one of the bright stars. Stella guessed this was their medicine man and was thankful when he'd finished. When he stepped to one side, the women and children joined in. Determined not to show she was afraid, Stella smiled and copied what they did. They sang and danced all night. When the sun was just peeping over the horizon, Rohanna took her hand and, with the women and children following, they danced away. Exhausted, Stella slipped into the bark shelter she shared with Rohanna and pulled a kangaroo skin over her tired body. Eyes drooping, she wondered why Dhakhan had brought her to this camp. He could easily have taken her home. Instead, he had brought her miles inland to an Aboriginal camp. There had to be a reason, but what it could be, she had no idea.

Chapter Twelve

From the seat in front of the cart, Ah Fong saw his mother stumble, noticed her bent shoulders. Concerned to see how weary she was, he wondered how long it would be before they reached the next waterhole. Suddenly the two donkeys raised their heads and brayed noisily. Dragging his eyes from his mother, he saw a huge dark ball speeding towards them, shutting out the sun. 'Father, mother, get on cart quick. Dust storm coming,' he shouted. In a few minutes the red dust had arrived. It blew in whirls around him, turning his hair and face red. His eyes smarted and he couldn't see where they were going, but the donkeys trusted him and he encouraged them to go forward into the swirls of dust. Holding the reins tight with one hand, he wiped the sleeve of his tunic across his sweating forehead. Wherever he looked the dust was there, swirling first in thick clouds, then in thin streams, but always shutting out his view of the track ahead.

Ah Fong pulled on the reins and managed to keep the donkeys steady, but he had no idea in which direction they were going. Glancing to his right, he saw through a thin strip of dust what seemed to be a sand dune. If he climbed up there, he might be able to see what lay ahead. 'Father, take reins. Mother stay on cart. I go see what over there,' he shouted and jumping down on to the red soil, ran towards the sand dune. Panting, he climbed to the top and looked down. Through the powdery dust he saw a few branches of trees waving in the stormy air. Where there were trees, it usually meant there was water.

'Father, Mother,' he shouted, running back to the cart. 'I think waterhole over there. We go that way,' he said, waving his hands in the direction of the sand dune. He was very thankful when, a short while later, they came to a shallow waterhole.

'We stay here tonight,' Ah Fong said, helping his mother down from the cart.

When they had made camp in the shelter of a few tall boulders that stood close to the waterhole, Ah Fong securely tied the two donkeys to a gnarled white ghost gum. He knew the value of the two animals and carefully brushed the red soil from their coats. 'Ying, Yang, you good donkeys today,' he said softly, stroking their heads. 'Ah Fong pleased with you.' As if they understood what he'd said, the donkeys brayed contentedly.

'Put tent here,' Ah Fong said to Wang helping his father.

Too weary to argue, Wang just nodded.

That night, Ah Fong, worried about his mother, found sleep difficult. However, the next morning when he saw the dust cloud had gone and the sky was clear, he began to feel a little better. Rubbing his sore eyes, he sat by the dying campfire and watched the sun rise. He would drive the cart that night, he decided, and when the stars came out, he would continue in a southerly direction towards the gold his father said would change their lives.

That night, alone with the stars, he couldn't help wondering what they would do if they didn't find the gold his father was so sure was there.

CHAPTER THIRTEEN

Days passed. The cart bumped and lurched along ruts of dry cracked earth. Sitting alone, reins loose in his hands, Ah Fong watched the horizon rise and fall as they made their way through the harsh outback. When they passed through a thicket of grey leaved bushes, he couldn't help comparing them to the rich green trees they had left behind in their village in China.

They never saw another person and the cart rumbled mile after mile over the parched red soil. Fence posts, with pale hawks perched on them, were the only signs they might be near a homestead or station where the cattlemen lived.

Once, they passed the gate of an Aboriginal camp. Ah Fong looked down the track behind the gate, but there was nobody there, just a solid line of ants stretching as far as he could see. When they passed an outcrop of weathered sandstone rocks with peaks twenty feet high, he wondered if they were the Aborigine sacred sites he'd heard so much about.

Eventually they came to a large billabong. Hot and thirsty, the donkeys rushed towards the water. Whilst they drank, Ah Fong refilled the water cans that hung along the sides of the cart. He dug a hole in the ground, lined it with stones and piled dried grass and bark into it. Then he rubbed together the two metal rods Hua had brought from China and made a fire. When it was glowing as red as the setting sun, he went to find his mother.

'Mother, fire is ready.' he called out.

'Thank you Ah Fong,' she called back. Then she screamed.

Dropping the stick he'd been using to stoke the fire, Ah Fong rushed over to where his mother was pointing at something, a look of horror on her face.

'What is matter?' he asked, then stopped and stared. Glistening in the late afternoon sunshine, a snake, nine feet long, was sliding towards them.

Ah Fong didn't stop to think, he jumped towards it, landing close, but the snake was faster and shot away. It was just about to disappear under a boulder, when the snake turned its head and, eyes glittering, looked straight at Ah Fong. 'I am Wallujabi and this is my Dreaming site,' the snake piped in a shrill voice. 'Why you come here?'

Ah Fong's knees trembled. Taking a deep breath he replied, 'We come from another land seeking the yellow rock they call gold.'

Wallujabi opened his mouth wide. 'Many come to find such rock and many die,' he hissed.

'We've been travelling many days. Do you know where the gold rock is?' Ah Fong asked, feeling a little more confident.

'The gold rock is of the earth. Why you want it?' Wallujabi asked.

'My father Wang want it. He say it will bring him many good things,' Ah Fong replied.

'I can take you to gold rock. You want go there?'

Ah Fong nodded. 'Can you take us to it?'

'Yes, but beware. Yellow rock bring danger,' Wallujabi piped, raising his face to the sky. 'Tomorrow at dawn, I will tell you where to find yellow rock,' and before Ah Fong could ask any further questions, he had slithered away.

'Father,' Ah Fong cried excitedly. 'A snake who says his name is Wallujabi, is going to take us to the gold.'

'A snake say that?' Wang laughed. 'Is true Hua?'

Hua looked at her husband and nodded. Then she walked over to the rock where Wallujabi had disappeared and spread out her washing.

The next morning, true to his word, Wallujabi re-appeared.

Ah Fong was already practising kung fu. Making a chopping movement with his hands, he looked down at the snake. 'Good morning Wallujabi,' he said solemnly. 'You come to tell us where to find the gold?'

'If that is what you still wish,' the snake hissed.

Ah Fong nodded. 'It is.'

'Go south for the next seven days. When you see the mountains, keep them on your right. Continue one more day. Then you will come to a place where there is a river. This has the yellow rock you seek. But, where the gold rock is, there is death,' he hissed and disappeared.

CHAPTER FOURTEEN

Stella passed her days in a haze of happiness. Every day she learnt more about the bush, its creatures and its plants. Rohanna showed her which plant or leaf she should use to cure headaches, which ones for stomach aches—the list grew longer each day.

Days in the sun darkened Stella's skin and bleached her hair until it was almost white. Every day she washed it in the billabong nearby and Rohanna showed her how to clean her teeth with a special piece of stick. One day, wearing a leather skirt Rohanna had given her, she was about to wash her dress, when she remembered the strike note Billy had given her. Slowly, she took out the crumpled paper and spread it out on the ground. The writing had smudged and the map was difficult to read. Barefooted, she ran over to where Rohanna sat preparing the evening meal. 'Rohanna,' she called, holding out the crumpled piece of paper. 'Do you know where this is?'

Rohanna looked at the paper then frowned. 'Where you get this?' she demanded.

Stella looked puzzled. 'It belonged to my pa. He was a prospector,' she answered, wondering why Rohanna was frowning.

As she continued to stare at the piece of paper, Rohanna's smile faded. 'This is land of the Aborigine. These rocks and cave are sacred place. You no go there,' she said.

'What do you mean I mustn't go there?'

'Danger there Stella. You no go there,' she insisted and putting the bread into the fire to cook, ran from the camp.

Stella watched her friend disappear. Why was the cave dangerous? Was it something her pa had done? Sad she'd made her new friend angry she decided not to mention the map again. Folding it up, she hid it under a dry rock.

From the shady side of the waterhole Dhakhan watched Stella learning to use the boomerang.

'You good now, Stella,' he laughed, picking up the boomerang and handing it to her.

Stella looked up, flapped her hand to get rid of the flies that had settled on her face and took the boomerang. 'Thanks Dhakhan. I haven't seen you for ages. Where've you been?

Dhakhan smiled back. 'I go many places, Stella of the Skies,' he said. 'And soon you go with new people—to your destiny.'

'My destiny?'

'Yes, soon you leave the Dimmajuba tribe and join other tribe. It comin' this way soon,' he said.

'But I don't want to go with another tribe. I'm happy here,' she replied. Annoyed and hurt by his words, she asked, 'Anyway, how do you know what my destiny is?'

'Dhakhan knows. Your destiny say you go with other people, but I will be by your side Stella. If you call me, I will come,' he said calmly.

'How do I know that Dhakhan?'

'Whisper Dhakhan three times, and you will see me.'

'Thanks,' Stella replied, regretting her thoughtless words. After all he had saved her from drowning and she knew she should be more grateful. 'So, where will I find this . . . other tribe?'

'In few days, they come this way. You will know them. They look for gold rock.'

'Will I be safe with them, Dhakhan?'

Dhakhan smiled and pointed to a tree behind her. 'Yes, you will be safe Stella, but I give you another friend. See, in the tree over there, my friend the dragon. He will look after you, warn you when there is danger.'

'Dragon? What do you mean dragon? There are no such things as dragons,' she stuttered, glancing nervously towards the tree.

'Yes, dragon there. See, he coming to you,' he said pointing to a lizard running down the tree trunk. 'He go red if there is danger and remember, Stella of the Skies, I come if you call,' he said gently, his brown body already disappearing.

Nervous, Stella watched the dragon skid to a stop at her feet, his ruff changing from green to orange.

'I am Stella, Stella of the Skies,' she said. Eyes wide open, the lizard looked at her. Patiently Stella waited to see what it would do. After a while the lizard jumped onto her wrist, ran up her arm and curled into a ball on her left shoulder.

Nervous, she put out her hand and touched it. It didn't move. 'You must have a name,' she said at last, staring at its tongue as it flicked in and out. Becoming more confident, she stroked the lizard between the eyes. 'I think I'll call you Jacko. Would you like that?'

Purring like a cat, the lizard closed its eyes.

'Jacko it shall be then,' she said and with Jacko still on her shoulder, walked back to the camp.

Chapter Fifteen

Dhakhan, Dhakhan, Dhakhan,' Stella whispered his name three times.

From a distance Dhakhan smiled and called back—

'Yes, Stella?'

'Where are you Dhakhan?

'I am with you Stella of the Skies.'

'B . . . but I can't see you. Where are you?' she asked, looking around.

'Look about you Stella.' His voice deep and dark echoed around the bare rocks.

Stella looked at the rocks and the deserted land 'I still can't *see* you,' she answered. 'I can only see kangaroos.'

'You not looking where I am,' Dhakhan replied, from the top of a red boulder.

'Oh there you are,' Stella cried looking upwards, surprised she hadn't noticed his muscular brown body before. 'Dhakhan, I need your help. You told me to call if I needed you and I need you now,' she pleaded. 'I don't want to go with the new tribe that's coming. I like Rohanna and I like being part of her tribe.'

For a long time Dhakhan scanned the horizon. 'Stella, your new family nearly here,' he said, appearing beside her.

'But Dhakhan, how do I know I'll be happy with these new people?' she asked, grabbing his arm.

'Oh, you will be happy—much happy,' he replied with a cheeky grin. 'Do not be afraid. Dhakhan watch out for you,' he said 'Look for me in the next bore hole,' he added. Then, giving her a wide smile, faded away.

Stella looked at the spot where he had disappeared. He hadn't told her anything about the tribe that was coming. Annoyed, she slowly returned to the camp fire where Rohanna was packing cooking utensils into a skin bag.

'Why are you going Rohanna? Why don't you stay and talk to these . . . er . . . new people?'

Rohanna shook her head. 'New people not Aborigine,' she said. 'They good people, but not Aborigine. Aborigine like to wander—they not need house—they have Mother earth—she give them food. We like hunt and search for berries and witchety grub,' she said laughing, remembering the look of horror on Stella's face when she had first seen her eating one. 'But, Stella, we friends. Believe and we will meet again . . .' she said, turning back to her work.

'Rohanna, how do you know all this? Stella asked. 'And why are you leaving me in the desert on my own?'

'You not alone Stella. New people nearly here,' Rohanna replied, continuing to pack.

It was not long before the tribe was ready to leave. Rohanna didn't say good-bye, she just turned and walked away joining the Elders who were leading the group into the desert.

Sad, Stella watched her friend disappear into the hazy mist of the desert. Then she turned her attention to the small dust ball on the horizon. Was this her destiny approaching? Alone and more than a little afraid, she waited.

CHAPTER SIXTEEN

As they travelled south, Ah Fong became stronger, his muscles hardened. He helped his mother because his father had said he must, but also because he could see her health was not good and he made sure he did the hard jobs like building a fire. He was very proud of his mother. In his village everybody had sought her help to cure their aches and pains and, if they were not able to pay for her services, they left gifts of rice and vegetables on the doorstep. Life was very different here—not a bit like his homeland, China.

Ah Fong scanned the horizon, seeking any sign that would tell him water was nearby. It had been several days since they had left the last waterhole and the water cans were almost empty. Now he wondered if he should have listened to the snake. From the top of a red sand dune, he gazed across the vast dusty countryside. Hot and thirsty, he wiped the perspiration from his face with the wide sleeve of his black jacket and slowly walked back to the cart. There he found his father resting in the shade of the cart with Hua beside him.

When Wang saw Ah Fong he started to moan. 'The sun, Ah Fong it make Hua sick. All day it beat on her head.'

'Yes father, that is because we travel south,' Ah Fong replied. 'Wallujabi said we should go south—that is where we will find the gold rock.'

Wang nodded. 'I hear what you say—we will go the way of the snake,' he said and bowing to his son, walked away.

So Ah Fong followed the snake's directions and steered the donkeys south to an area where few people lived.

CHAPTER SEVENTEEN

When Billy woke again the wagon had stopped and it was almost dark. Sad and troubled by the news that his ma and Stella were dead, he wondered what he should do. Peering into the dusk, he could see Zach and Ned sitting by the camp fire, a billycan hanging in its flames. Behind them four bullocks drank noisily at a waterhole. Clambering from the wagon, he stumbled over to the camp fire.

'Any tea in the billy?' he asked, licking his dry lips.

'Sure,' Ned said, reaching for another tin mug. Without speaking, he filled it with strong tea and handed it to Billy. 'There you are lad, drink that—it'll make you feel better.'

Billy took the mug, gulping the hot sweet tea. 'I've been thinking,' he said, at last. 'Now I got nobody, ma and Stella being dead like, maybe I could join up with you, if you want. Maybe have a sort of partnership?'

'Well, I don' know about a partnership Billy 'cos you already owes us the strike note,' Zach replied, coming straight to the point. 'Before you hit the bottle, you told us you'd read your pa's note so many times you knew it like the back of your hand. So, I'm thinking, if you take us to the place where ol' man Tom's gold is, maybe we could come to some sort of arrangement. What do you say Ned?' he said, winking slyly behind Billy's back.

'Well Billy, as Zach says, if you takes us to ol' man Tom's strike, maybe we could come to an arrangement,' he agreed slyly, unwilling to say what that arrangement might be. 'At the moment, you've got nothing. It's been two weeks since the cyclone and we've been looking out for you all that time, so you owe us Billy.'

Billy looked at Zach then Ned. Ned was a kind man, but he couldn't trust him and he certainly didn't trust Zach, but he couldn't do without them.

After a moment's thought he suggested hopefully, 'Maybe we could go to Tennant Creek instead? I've heard there's gold there.'

'Maybe, but first you gotta show us where ol' man Tom's gold is,' Zach insisted.

'OK,' Billy said giving in. 'I'll see if I can find pa's strike.'

'Let's shake on our agreement then shall we?' Zach said, putting out his hand. 'It's getting late now and we need to make an early start, so, as you been sleeping all day Billy, you can take first watch. Keep it sharp now, those Aborigines will steal from under your nose if you're not careful and remember Billy, I alus sleep with one eye open, so I'll be watching you,' and with that he pulled a blanket over his head and went to sleep.

Billy put more wood on the fire and gazed up at the thousands and thousands of stars scattering the inky black sky. In the distance a dingo howled. He shivered. Picking a stick from the fire, he drew a picture. He put in a river, some boulders, then added a few trees. His father had told him, just as he was leaving, that one of the gum trees had been split by lightning and that was how Billy would know he was in the right place. Billy stared at his drawing in the sand. Suddenly he remembered his father's note—*Beware the cave. It kills everybody who goes into it.* Billy didn't know what that meant, but he drew a cave opening in the rocks anyway. Then alone under the desert moon, he made a vow. 'I'll find your strike pa, I promise,' he whispered.

Chapter Eighteen

Ah Fong jumped from rock to rock looking for a waterhole. Suddenly he saw something that made him stop and blink. He closed his eyes and looked again. The figure was still there, sitting on top of a sandstone rock. Sunlight shimmered on yellow hair. He shook his head—not Aborigine—Aborigines had black hair.

Determined to find out more, he crept closer.

The figure was a girl. She had golden hair and was stroking a lizard. Ah Fong's heart began to beat rapidly. He covered his eyes with his hands, counted to ten and opened them again. Watching her yellow hair blowing in the hot breeze, he thought she was the most beautiful thing he'd ever seen. Hiding behind a silver gum, he picked up a small pebble and threw it in her direction. The desert was still and the pebble landed with a noisy plonk, scattering the noisy galahs perched on a branch above his head. The girl didn't move. He crept a bit closer. When he was close enough to see the fair eyelashes that swept across her cheek, he picked up another pebble. This time it landed in her lap.

The lizard lifted its head in alarm; its frill turned from green to orange. Sensing danger, it ran up the girl's arm. Perched on her shoulder, it jerked its head back and forth, letting out strange squeaking noises.

Ah Fong saw the girl laugh, then stroke the lizard's neck. 'Hello,' he called softly.

There was no reply.

After a moment, he called again, louder this time—still no reply. Perhaps she was deaf and couldn't hear. Holding his bamboo pole defensively in front of him, he stepped cautiously out from behind the gum tree. When he got to the rock where she sat, he stood in front of her, bowed politely and said, 'Hello, me Ah Fong.'

'Why have you been throwing pebbles at me?' the girl demanded, staring in surprise at the Chinese boy, taking in his black trousers, high necked jacket and pigtail.

'Me Ah Fong,' he said again, a wide smile stretching from ear to ear.

The girl stood up, took a step towards him.

'Hi, I'm Stella,' she said, holding out her hand.

Ah Fong nodded and smiled. Not knowing what to say, he decided to get his mother. 'I go get Hua, my Mother,' he said and ran towards the cart that was rumbling towards them.

'Mama come quick. I find girl,' Ah Fong called, dashing up the three steps at the back of the cart. Peering inside, he found his mother lying on the makeshift bed.

'Mama what wrong, you sick?'

'No Ah Fong, hot. What you want?' she asked, holding a wet cloth to her forehead.

'Mama, I find girl. Please come, speak with her,' he said, holding out his hand.

'You find what?' his mother questioned, raising her head in surprise.

'I find girl, Mama,' he announced dramatically.

'Where her family? She Aborigine?'

'No not Aborigine. Hair yellow,' Ah Fong declared. 'Come Mama, I show you,' he said and taking her hand dragged her outside.

'Look, she over there,' he said, pointing at Stella sitting on the rock in the shade of a lone gum tree.

Hua peered through the shimmering heat at the girl. Headache forgotten, she smiled for the first time in many days.

CHAPTER NINETEEN

Over the next weeks Billy's face and body tanned to a deep brown and his hands hardened. He liked looking after the bullocks. He took each one in turn, sitting on their backs and riding them until he gained their trust. He called the leading male Zorro and his mate, Bessie. He had difficulty telling the other two apart, but as one had a small white patch on her back, he simply called her Patch and the other Daisy. Every evening he wiped the sweat from their backs, cleaned the dust from their eyes and it was not long before they began to take food from his hand. One evening he noticed Zach fumbling with the reins. 'Would you like me to do that Zach?' he asked.

Surprised, Zach looked up. 'Why that's good of you boy. They're a bit restless tonight. I heard a dingo howling a while back—that always makes 'em jittery,' he said, lashing the whip across Zorro's back, trying to make the bullock stand still.

'OK, I'll see to them,' Billy replied, snatching the reins from Zach's shaking hands. 'Steady boy,' he said to Zorro, scratching him gently between the horns. Immediately Zorro stopped stamping and snorted softly in reply.

Zach stared at Billy in amazement. 'You certainly got a way wi' them bullocks,' he admitted grudgingly.

'I like animals,' Billy agreed. Turning to the other three bullocks, he gave them all a scratch. 'I wouldn't mind looking after them all the time if you like.'

'It's a big responsibility, Billy. If we lost the bullocks, we'd all most likely die, you know that, don' you?'

'Yes, I know that,' Billy answered.

'OK, I'll have a word with Ned.'

'Thanks,' Billy muttered. 'It'd mean you'd have less to do when we made camp,' he called after Zach's retreating figure.

Zach didn't answer. He was trying to think of a way to cut Billy out of the gold strike.

Early the next morning Billy was preparing the bullocks for the day ahead when he saw Zach strolling towards him.

'I 'ad a word with Ned last night,' Zach said. 'He's noticed 'ow you likes the bullocks. So, we decided you could give it a go, see 'ow you get on,' he said gruffly and without another word, turned on his heel and left.

Billy watched him go. Zach and Ned had both been swagmen, arriving at homesteads on foot and he wondered how the bullocks had got into their possession? He suspected they'd won the wagon and the bullocks at the gambling table. If they had, it meant they didn't know much about livestock so it didn't take Billy long to work out that he was a very important part in their survival. Not only did he know where the strike was, but he also had control of the bullocks.

Billy studied the bullocks, what they did and how they adjusted to the harshness of the outback. He noticed, when they were close to a waterhole, their ears would flatten and they would start to bellow. The next time he saw them do that, he let the reins loose so they could find their own way to the water. One evening, however, for no reason that Billy could think of, they suddenly changed direction and galloped in a westerly direction dragging the wagon over the hard rutted track making it sway dangerously.

'Pull them bullocks in, Billy.' Zach's angry voice echoed out from inside the wagon. 'The wheels will come off if you're not more careful.'

'Sorry Zach,' Billy shouted over his shoulder, gradually getting the animals back under control and pulling the wagon to a halt. 'The bullocks could smell water—so I let them go for it.'

'Well make sure they don' do it again,' Zach's angry voice shouted back.

Billy was angry with himself. He'd have to be more careful in future. He didn't want Zach taking over the bullocks again. The more he thought about the bullocks, the more determined he became to find a way to understand them, but not with force—that was Zach's way. The question was, how? That, he would have to learn.

CHAPTER TWENTY

Billy held the bullocks in check and gazed across the empty dried land. It was almost evening and the sun was rapidly disappearing beneath the horizon. He licked his dry lips. His eyes gazed longingly at the water cans hanging along the side of the wagon. They were nearly empty. Frowning with worry, he searched for a sign that would tell him water was nearby.—a clump of gum trees or birds circling in the sky perhaps, but there was nothing. If they didn't find water soon, they would be in real trouble.

'You'll have to be extra careful in the night Billy,' Zach said that evening when they were sitting by the campfire. 'We don't want to wake up in the morning and find the bullocks gone. The Aborigines are quite happy to kill the white man's beast.' He gave a half laugh and stirred the fire so it burnt more brightly. 'A bullock makes good eating for the whole tribe an' since you've taken on the responsibility fer 'em, you'd best be watchful.'

Billy only half listened. He knew how important the bullocks were and didn't need Zach to keep telling him what to do. When he was alone at night he would keep himself wide awake by studying the stars. Most of all, he liked to pick out the group of stars called the Southern Cross—the stars that would lead him south to his father's strike. Also he knew, if he ever got lost, the stars would guide him through the desert.

CHAPTER TWENTY-ONE

Under a cloudless sky, Zach stretched out under the leafy branches of a ghost gum and thought about the fine horse he'd get when he got his hands on ol' Tom's strike. He'd also have a leather saddle made and get some of those leather chaps the gentlemen wore.

'No rain again Zach,' Ned interrupted his thoughts.

'Yeah, I know,' Zach drawled, annoyed at having his daydream spoilt. 'What's this crazy idea Billy's got—that them bullocks'll find water if you let them go where they want. I ain' so sure about that, but it's three days now since we came across a waterhole.'

'So what are you saying we should do?'

'I don' know yet. 'Ave a word with Billy. See if he's got something in mind.'

'OK, but I don't hold out much hope he'll be able to suggest anything,' Ned replied, heading off to find Billy.

Zach stretched out again, closed his eyes. A slight rustle made his hand flash towards his leg, but he was too late, a black python snake had already curled its body around his hand. Stiff with fear, he stared at the snake. The snake held his eyes. Suddenly it opened its mouth wide and hissed, 'I am Wallujabi, Spirit of the Snake and guardian of waterholes. You seek water?'

'I . . . We, yes the buffalo need water,' Zach stuttered.

'And . . .'

Zach looked down at the snake curled around his hand, wondering how he could get rid of it. Not sure what the snake had meant, he finally said, 'We're prospectors looking for gold.'

Unblinking, Wallujabi's head swayed back and forth. 'I know yellow rock. Where you look for it?' he hissed.

'If you get off my hand, I'll draw the spot for you,' Zach replied angrily.

Wallujabi nodded and slowly unwound its coils from Zach's hand.

'Can you take us to this place?' Zach asked, drawing a picture of Billy's map in the sand.

For a long moment, the snake stared at the drawing. Then, he hissed. 'Perhaps, I take you this place, but first you get water.'

'And then?' Zach asked.

'You will see,' the snake replied and swiftly slithered across the ground and vanished beneath a boulder.

Zach shook his head, staring at the spot where the snake had disappeared. Why had it agreed so readily? Something was not right. He'd have to be more careful—you couldn't trust a snake—of that he was quite sure.

CHAPTER TWENTY-TWO

The red, gold and black painted cart covered in Chinese writing rattled along the dusty track, the tiny bags hanging along its sides dancing in rhythm to the wheels.

Stella stared at the tiny woman hurrying towards her. 'Me Hua,—Medicine Woman and these—my cures for pain,' she said pointing at the bags. 'All different—these for pain in stomach—these for pain in head. All bag for different pain.'

Stella smiled back. 'So . . . where are you going?' she asked.

'Wang look for yellow rock,' Hua said.

Stella's heart flipped. Gold—they were looking for gold. Smiling, trying not to show her interest, she said, 'Me medicine woman too. I learn of the things out here that can cure pain,' she said, waving her hand in the direction of the scrub bushes. Her heart twisted for a moment as she remembered the happy days she and Rohanna had had collecting leaves and wild plants to make potions for her tribe. But since that time was over, she pushed all thoughts of her friend out of her mind.

'Many peoples need good medicine woman,' Hua said. 'Perhaps Ste . . . l . . . la help me?' she asked, stumbling over the name.

Not sure what to say, Stella crumbled the dry leaves in one of the bags. 'My friend Rohanna showed me which berries and leaves to use to cure headaches and stomach aches and many other things. They are all out there,' she said, waving her hand again in the direction of the bush.

'Rohanna? Who Rohanna?' Hua asked.

'Rohanna is an Aborigine girl with the Wanujabbi tribe. I've been living with them. But they've gone walkabout and now I have no-one.'

'We go to Tennant Creek,' Hua said. 'You come with us?'

Stella hesitated. Should she join the Chinese family, she wondered? She looked into the distance. There was nobody else. It seemed, she didn't have a choice.

'Maybe we make good medicine together,' Hua continued. 'You no family now Aborigine gone. You travel with us?'

Stella put up her hand and stroked Jacko's neck. 'What do you think we should do Jacko?

Jacko slid down her arm and settled firmly on her hand. Stella stared at him. 'Well?'

Eyes wide, Jacko looked up. His frilled neck turned blue.

'So, you think it'll be all right?' Stella guessed, remembering that Dhakhan had said red was the colour for danger.

Jacko flicked out his tongue and licked her finger. Stella laughed softly and stroked his head with her other hand. 'Thank you. We'll go with you to Tennant Creek,' she agreed and, taking Hua's outstretched hand, walked over to the cart where Ah Fong was waiting.

CHAPTER TWENTY-THREE

'This is Jacko. He likes you,' Stella said, holding out her arm.

'How you know that?' Ah Fong asked.

'See his ruff,' she said, pointing at the lizard. 'It's a sort of blue—that means he likes you. If he didn't like you his ruff would go red or orange—that would mean danger and I should stay away.'

Ah Fong laughed. 'Well Stella, if Jacko like me I will show you my friends, Ying and Yang,' he said running over to the donkeys, running his hands down their backs. 'Donkeys very strong. You like hold reins?' he asked.

Stella nodded and climbed on to the thin plank of wood in front of the cart. Nervous, she clucked her tongue. 'Giddy-up,' she called softly. The donkeys didn't move. 'Ying, Yang, come on off we go,' she shouted more loudly.

Standing by the donkeys, Ah Fong whispered in Ying's ear. Suddenly they shot forward, racing over the red dusty soil. Stella pulled on the reins. 'Whoa,' she cried, clinging to the seat. The donkeys charged on. 'Ying Yang, stop, stop,' she cried, but the donkeys didn't seem to hear.

Laughing, Ah Fong grabbed the reins out of Stella's hands. 'Look I show you how,' he said and pulling hard on the rein attached to Ying's yoke pulled the cart to a halt. 'Ying is man donkey,' he said, as if that explained everything.

A frown crossed Stella's face. Man donkey indeed. 'Give me a few weeks and I'll show you I can manage the donkeys as well as you can,' she declared defiantly.

In the afternoon when they came to a small waterhole, they all agreed they should set up camp there. Ah Fong made a fire and Hua began to cook a light meal of rice and dumplings. Finding there was not much she could do to help, Stella sat in the shade and waited for the food to be cooked. Immediately her thoughts turned to her mother. Was she in Darwin with Billy? If they were together, did they talk about her, wonder where she was? Secretly she longed to see her family, but she tried not to think about it too often because it always made her feel sad. Putting on a bright face, she looked at Ah Fong talking to the donkeys. He was kind and Wang and Hua had taken her into their family. Eventually they would get to a town and she'd get a lift with a drover back to Darwin. Pleased with the plan, she settled on the warm earth and pulled up a blanket. Comforted by the low murmur of Wang and Hua talking in the background, her eyelids drooped and she fell asleep.

She was climbing a cliff. The air was thin—breathing was difficult. The sun beat on the red rock; heat burst through her shoes. But she could see the top—it wasn't far. Suddenly a face appeared over the edge—Dhakhan was smiling down at her. Leaning forward, he took her small hand in his, hauled her to safety. Gasping for breath, she looked out over the plains. In the distance, she could see the roofs of a sprawling shanty town glittering in the sunshine.

'Your new world Stella of the Skies,' Dhakhan said. 'Here you find happiness.'

'What do you mean?' she asked, but another voice was calling 'Stella, Stella.'

She opened her eyes and Hua was smiling down at her. 'Wake up, Stella. Time for food,' she said.

CHAPTER TWENTY-FOUR

Billy gazed towards the inland lake half hidden behind the sand dunes. The bullocks, already smelling water, were charging towards it. Suddenly Zorro stopped and reared up.

'What's the matter my friend?' Billy cried, pulling on the reins, but as he spoke he saw the reason—a black python was uncurling in the track ahead. Billy knew a python's venom was not poisonous, but it could squeeze the life from a man or beast very quickly, so he picked up a stick and was just about to hit the snake, when he heard Zach calling.

'Billy, leave the snake alone,' Zach shouted, running towards the snake. 'It won't harm you if you don't touch it.'

'But . . .

'I said, leave it alone,' Zach shouted again, raising his fist in anger.

'All right, all right, if you say so. I was only thinking of the bullocks,' Billy said, stroking Zorro behind the ears, calming him.

'Billy, you know nothing about the outback. When I tell you not to do something, you don't do it, d'you hear me?'

'OK, OK,' Billy replied soothingly. Not understanding why Zach was so angry, he shrugged his shoulders and started to walk towards the other bullocks. Suddenly the snake moved. Billy's grip on the stick tightened. Eyes narrowed, he watched the snake slither towards him. Eyes flared with fear, the bullocks bellowed noisily. Keeping calm, Billy turned and walked away from Zach and the bullocks—the snake followed. He looked over his shoulder—it was getting closer. It was a weird feeling. He'd never been followed by a snake before.

Suddenly the snake stopped. Opening its mouth, it hissed, 'I am Wallujabi—I am from the Dreamtime.'

'Wh . . . what do you mean from the Dreamtime?' Billy asked, his voice trembling.

The snake slithered nearer. 'The rock you seek. The one called gold. It bring danger and harm. Why you look for it?'

'Because . . .' Billy hesitated, then decided to tell the snake the real reason. 'Because my father was a prospector and I'm looking for his gold strike,' he replied, getting ready to hit the snake if it got too close. 'He told me to look in a cave.'

'I know the cave you seek,' the snake hissed.

'You do? Can you take me to it?' Billy asked eagerly, forgetting his fear.

'I can, but there is a price.'

'What do you mean—a price?'

'That, you will find out,' Wallujabi repeated and, tongue flicking angrily, slithered away. When it was a short distance from the rocks where it had first appeared, it stopped. Head weaving, it hissed, 'Well? Do you agree?'

Billy stared at the snake then nodded. 'I agree,' he said slowly.

Satisfied, the snake disappeared.

For a while Billy thought about what the snake had said. He wouldn't tell Zach, not this time. He knew how much Zach wanted the gold, but the snake, what did it want? For a while he puzzled over the question. If the snake knew where the cave was, why shouldn't he let it lead them to it?

From his hideout, Wallujabi watched Billy watering the bullocks. White fella brought trouble to his land and his people, especially those who sought the yellow rock. He, Wallujabi, would take these white fellas to the cave, but they would pay the price. His eyes slid round, fell on the wagon. He quivered in excitement—that would be a good place to hide. He waited until Zach and Ned were talking quietly by the fire, then slithered silently up the steps into the wagon and hid under a pile of blankets.

Later that night he was woken by whispering. In the lantern's half light, he could see Zach and Ned playing the two penny game - Two Up. Unseen, he listened—

'When we get to the cave, we'll drop a little of this in Billy's tea,' Zach said, waving a small bag in the air. 'It'll make him sleep. Then, we'll take him into the desert—leave him there.'

'But Zach, we can't do that,' Ned stuttered.

'Why not? You don't want Billy claiming the gold do you?'

'No . . .'

'Well then, keep quiet and leave everything to me. Now get some sleep. We've got a big day tomorrow,' he said, blowing out the lantern.

Unseen, Wallujabi slid back under the blankets.

CHAPTER TWENTY-FIVE

Stella searched the parched land for the plant Rohanna had said was good for headaches. Out of the corner of her eye she could see Ah Fong's black jacket outlined against the blue sky, a long pole hanging from his waist. Curious, she forgot the plants and ran over to where he was standing.

'What are you doing?' she asked, watching him carry out complicated hand and foot movements.

'I do southern dragon kung fu,' he replied proudly.

'What's that?'

'Martial art of my family—see—' he said, pulling back the wide sleeve of his jacket, showing off a blue and red dragon tattoo circling his arm and wrist. 'In China, dragon water spirit bring rain for farmer. Chinese people bow to dragon—he have great wisdom.'

'Really?' she spluttered, wanting to tell him she had a dragon, but deciding against it. Instead she asked, 'What's that you're holding?'

'This is king dragon heart piercing pole,' he replied, holding it out for her to look at it.

'And what do you do with it when you're not chasing dragons?' she laughed.

'Ah Fong work hard—get to high level soon. kung fu mean long practice,' he said his face serious.

'Could I learn?' Stella asked.

'Yes, Stella. Kung fu good for woman too. You come early, I show you. Now I must go—do kung fu on rock up there,' he said.

Stella stood and watched him climb the rock, then returned to the spot where she thought the headache plant might be. Life in the outback was hard, she thought bending to pick a flower. It might be a good thing if she knew how to look after herself.

The next day, eager to learn Ah Fong's martial art, Stella was up early.

Ah Fong saw her coming, put his hands together and bowed in greeting. 'Good morning, Stella. Today you learn self defence Chinese way?'

'Can't wait,' she answered, kicking out with her foot.

'No Stella. First you learn to move your foots, like this,' he said, laughing, showing her what to do.

'Don't laugh Ah Fong. I really do want to do this,' she said, trying to copy him.

'Very well, Stella, but first you learn defence,' he said.

Stella ducked as his hand swung towards her shoulder. Instinctively she spun round, but he was already twirling on his feet, pinning her against the rock.

Ah Fong grinned. 'You have quick brain Stella, but you must move foots as well. Come I show you again.'

'OK, but one day I'll beat you,' she laughed.

Chapter Twenty-Six

The sun beat mercilessly on the dry earth. From the shade of a gum, Stella squinted into the bright light and watched the red-grey ball grow bigger. When she saw something flash in the sunlight, a warning bell rang. Slowly, she walked over to Wang who was standing beside the donkeys. 'I think this might be Rangers,' she said.

'Rangers? Who Rangers?' Wang asked.

'Uhm, well a Ranger is a kind of policemen, but don't worry I had to deal with the police many times when Billy got into trouble. I'll talk to them,' she added quietly but firmly.

'No like police,' Wang replied, worry lines showing on his tired face.

'Don't worry Wang. I'll soon send them on their way,' she said. Worried, she fixed her eyes on the dust ball and waited for the Rangers to arrive.

Three men reined in their horses, spat dust from their mouths. The tallest jumped out of the saddle and flashed his badge.

'Good afternoon, Officer. What can we do for you?' Stella asked, politely.

Ah Fong, Hua and Wang waited silently by the cart.

'Good afternoon Miss,' the Officer said, taking off his wide-brimmed hat. 'You're a long way from town. Where're you heading?' he asked, giving her a long hard look. 'The outback's a dangerous place—especially for someone as young as you. Are these friends of yours?'

'Yes, they are. I've been travelling with them for some time now. We're heading south to Tennant Creek. 'Wang . . .' she waved a hand in his direction, 'is interested in buying a stake out at the gold site. This is Hua, his wife, and Ah Fong his son. Hua is a medicine woman and would like to set up a clinic.'

'Would she now,' the second policeman said, a disapproving tone in his voice. 'People are a bit suspicious of the Chinese out here. Have they got a permit to dig?'

'Yes, they got a permit before they left Darwin and I do know how people feel,' Stella replied defensively. 'Wang, show him your permit,' she said, taking the piece of paper Wang took from the sleeve of his tunic. 'I'm from Darwin too. They saved my life in the cyclone,' she lied.

'And where are your parents?'

'My pa was a prospector—he died out in the desert. I want to go to Tennant Creek to see if anybody knows anything about him. I don't know what happened to my ma. She disappeared when the cyclone hit Aunt Edna's house and I . . . I never saw her again.'

'What's your name?'

'Stella Whitney,' she answered briefly.

'Whitney,' he muttered, trying to recall the name amongst those reported missing after the cyclone. 'All right, Stella, you and your friends can go on your way now. When I get back to Darwin, I'll see if I can find out anything about your ma. Oh, and you'd better report to the police station when you get to Tennant Creek. Just so as we know you're OK,' he added.

Stella nodded.

Whilst the Officer was writing in his notebook, she cast a glance at the Aborigine policeman. In the shade of his wide brimmed hat she could see he was smiling. He was a bit like . . . 'Dhakhan?' she said out loud, but he'd already turned away as if he hadn't heard. Disappointed, she reached up to touch Jacko who was curled around the back of her neck. Half asleep, his head drooped over her shoulder, but his ruff was blue, so she guessed everything was OK. 'I think Hua's cures will be welcomed by the prospectors or at least by their wives and I'm going to help her,' she informed the policeman, making sure he understood they were all going to work when they got to Tennant Creek.

'There's a Flying Doctor Service that's just started in Alice. That'll take care of any serious matters, but prospectors' wives might welcome help with everyday aches and pains,' the second police officer said, mopping the perspiration from his forehead.

'Well, if that's all Officer, we'll be moving on,' Stella said, ignoring his comments.

'By the way, we passed two other families travelling down to Tennant Creek. They are over in that direction,' the Officer in charge said waving his hand eastwards. 'It might be safer if you all travelled together. I'll ride over and tell them you're here if you like.'

'How many miles is it to Tennant Creek, Officer?'

'Well you've just passed Powell Creek, so that makes Tennant Creek about another 75 miles or so down the track that way,' he said, pointing south.

'Well since we've come this far and we don't know what the other people are like, I think we can manage to get the rest of the way on our own.' Taking the reins from Ah Fong's hands, she shouted, 'Giddy up.'

Obediently the donkeys trotted forward.

'Well, you've certainly got some guts, I'll say that for you,' the Officer in charge said, riding alongside the cart. After a short distance, he turned his horse round and prepared to leave. 'By the way, when you get to the Creek, just tell 'em Jack sent you. They'll know who that is,' he said with an easy laugh.

'I will Officer and thank you again,' Stella replied, a disturbing knot in her stomach. As they disappeared in a cloud of dust, she wondered why they had come? Was it just routine or was there another reason? For a brief moment her thoughts lingered on Billy, then her ma. Were they still in Darwin? Or was Billy already looking for the strike? She wished she knew.

Four days later, as a red sun was peeping over the horizon, Stella, eager to continue with her kung fu training, clambered up a large boulder. The fresh air made her feel good. Stopping halfway to get her breath, she couldn't help gazing at the unusual rocks scattered over the landscape. Some of them were so smooth and round they looked like large pebbles. Pulling the map from the pocket she had sewn in her dress, she checked her father's drawing. They looked very similar, but rocks were rocks and it was impossible to be sure. Carefully she folded the map and returned it to the secret pocket.

CHAPTER TWENTY-SEVEN

Billy glared at the scaly black head and glossy dark brown body gliding towards him and shuddered. He didn't like snakes, but determined to find out what the snake knew, he waited until it had almost reached his feet, then asked, 'We've been travelling for two weeks Wallujabi, when are we going to get to the cave?'

'Soon,' Wallujabi hissed, his small black eyes flickering here and there, never settling anywhere.

'Well if it ain't our guide Wallujabi.' Zach sneered, walking over to the snake. Curling his lip, he spat at a nearby stone, narrowly missing its head. 'We haven't seen you for ages. Where've you been?'

Wallujabi didn't flinch, but his eyes narrowed dangerously. 'I am Dreaming Spirit of the Black-headed Python and I go everywhere,' he answered, flicking his tongue angrily. 'Tonight, you must follow the southern cross and tomorrow at dawn you will see the Dreaming of my Spiritual ancestors.'

'Where?' Billy asked, his voice rising in excitement.

'At the two tall rocks. Go through them and you will come to the cave and what you seek, but beware the Dreamtime. It will be all around you,'

Billy stared at the snake and remembered his father's warning. Was Wallujabi also trying to warn him?

That night, as Wallujabi had suggested, they continued going south. As the stars began to fade, Billy yawned. Then he squinted, leaned forward, the reins tight in his hands. In the early morning mist, two ghostly pillars floated into view. A feeling of fear and hope swept through him. 'Zach, Zach,' he called, his voice shrill with excitement. 'Come and look at this!'

Zach's tousled head appeared out of the wagon.

'It's the pillars Zach. The ones Wallujabi mentioned.'

With a thump, Zach sat down beside Billy at the front of the wagon. 'You think these are the pillars your father drew on his map?' he asked.

'Well, they look something like them,' Billy agreed. More cautiously, he added, 'To me they look like the entrance to something. I think we should drive through them as Wallujabi suggested and see where they lead. And we don't want to go off the track. There're too many jagged rocks out there,' he said, spreading his arms wide.

Suddenly, for no apparent reason, the bullocks began to snort and holler.

'Yeah, the track seems to go between the pillars,' Zach agreed, trying to ignore the bullocks.

Billy nodded. He was about to add something when he was interrupted by Ned appearing at the flaps of the wagon. 'What's the matter with them bullocks?' he shouted. 'Why are they making all that noise?'

'This is not the time to be worrying about them Ned, come and look at this,' Zach shouted, pointing at the pillars.

Buttoning up his trousers, Ned stumbled out of the wagon, his eyes following Zach's outstretched arms. 'Well,' he drawled. 'Looks like the snake was right. He said we'd come to an entrance. But we don't know what's beyond there, so I think we should stop and brew some tea before we go in.'

'You're right Ned,' Billy agreed, pulling the bullocks to a halt. Jumping down, he walked over to them, patting and stroking their sweating heads. Why were they so noisy this morning, he wondered? A gut feeling told him things were not going to be as easy as they looked. When Zach was not looking, he made sure they had extra feed and water.

Chapter Twenty-Eight

Days and nights ran into each other and it was still dark when Wang took the reins from Stella's stiff fingers. 'You sleep now,' he said gently.

Exhausted, Stella sank onto the makeshift bed on the cart. A minute later she was asleep.

'Stella, wake up.' Ah Fong shook her shoulder. 'Come,' he said urgently. 'I t'ink we at Tennant Creek.

Yawning, Stella stumbled into the sunlight. Shading the sun from her tired eyes, she looked around and gasped in surprise. The dry dusty earth had gone. The cart stood in the middle of green pasture land. Below, a small settlement nestled in a valley. People as small as ants crossed and re-crossed the only street.

A short distance from the settlement, a river sparkled in the morning sunlight. Twisting and turning, it wound its way towards the shade of a mountain range. Higher up the river, a wooden wheel was dredging water and gravel from the river bed. Although still early, it was already hot and several prospectors, wearing large brimmed hats, were heading towards the river. Those who had reached the shallow area were panning the gravel, sifting through the pebbles and stones, praying this would be the day they found gold.

Everywhere she looked there was hustle and bustle.

'Well, it looks as though this is the place we're looking for—let's go and find out what we have to do,' she said, grinning broadly at Wang.

Wang didn't need any encouragement. 'Hua, pack quickly,' he shouted. 'We go now—find gold.'

Head high, Stella drove the donkeys down the middle of the street. The people there were used to strangers, but they couldn't help staring at the tousled blonde girl driving two donkeys pulling a brightly painted cart and the Chinese family trudging wearily behind.

Ignoring their curious glances, Stella pulled up beside two horses tied to a tethering rail. Jumping down, she straightened her dusty dress and walked up to a woman walking in the shade of the long verandah.

'Excuse me, this is Tennant Creek isn't it? And . . . er . . . could you tell me where the Register Office is?' she asked, her voice squeaky with excitement.

The lady nodded her head knowingly. She had met many people who'd asked the same question, but this girl and her companions were not the usual types.

'No dearie, this ain't Tennant Creek. The Creek's down that way,' she said, pointing to a dry rutted track leading out of town. 'But there's mining here and if it's gold you're looking for, you've come to the right place.'

'Good, so where do we go to get registered?' Stella asked.

Ignoring her question, the woman said, 'My name's Martha and I run this establishment,' she said proudly pointing her parasol at the building behind her. 'Oh, but you want the Registry Office don't you. It's at the end of town. But you look worn out dearie, where's your ma and pa?'

'They're dead. My pa died in the desert—he was a prospector you know—name of Albert Whitney,' Stella said proudly. 'You heard of him?'

The woman shook her head.

'I don't know where my ma is,' Stella continued, 'These people,' she indicated Wang, Hua and Ah Fong, 'saved my life in the floods that hit Darwin. They've been very good to me. The end of town you say. I can see a red building down there. Is that the one you mean?'

The woman nodded. 'I run the only hotel here and I know most of the people, so you if you have any problems, come and see me,' she said kindly and, flipping her skirt out behind her, walked into the saloon.

Stella watched the woman disappear, then turned to where Wang was waiting. 'This is not Tennant Creek I'm afraid, but there's mining here and you can register a stake at the office at the end of the strcet. Do you want to do that?'

Wang nodded. 'We go make claim, now, Stella.'

'OK, here we go then,' she laughed lightly and taking up the reins guided the donkeys down the dusty street to the Registry Office.

Two weeks later, Stella climbed to the top of one of the huge boulders and looked over the tops of the tents pitched on the red parched land beside the river. The heat was terrifying, but away from the camp and its overpowering stench of cooking, the air was cleaner and there was a light breeze. Settling against the warm bare rock, she looked down on the barren landscape and began to think about her mother, then Billy, wondering where they were and what they might be doing. She sighed. She couldn't do anything about them at the moment, but amongst all these prospectors, there must be somebody who'd known her father or perhaps heard of him. She stared out at the red evening sky and the band of kangaroos hopping on the skyline. Night came quickly in the desert and the darkening sky reminded her she must go and meet Wang. The Australian prospectors hadn't taken kindly to the Chinese family, but they seemed to like her, so to make sure they all got home safely, she arranged to meet Wang and Ah Fong at the river's edge. Clambering from the rock, she hurried back to the river. Tired from a day's hard work, she found them sitting on a small piece of grass, waiting patiently for her to arrive. Smiling, she helped Wang to his feet and keeping them both close beside her, guided them through the debris to the outskirts of the camp where Hua was preparing the evening meal. After they had eaten, Stella returned to the river and bathed. Refreshed, she combed her long blonde hair and listened to the gossip. It was always the same—the lucky ones who had found gold.

Despite a few protests, Hua and Stella set up a clinic outside their tent. On a white board Stella wrote:

HUA'S CLINIC
ACHES AND PAINS CURED
WOUNDS STITCHED
OPEN—8.00—11.00 AM
PLEASE QUEUE HERE

Word about the clinic spread quickly. It was usually women who wanted Hua's advice and it was not long before the Clinic became a meeting place. One day, when two women in the queue were gossiping, Stella's sharp ears heard the word cave. Pretending to work, she listened to their conversation.

'You know young Jimmy Brown?

'Yes, I know him. Why do you ask?'

'Well, I heard he went up to the Dreaming Cave—you know the Aboriginal burial site and when he came out, he'd gone mad. So mad, it seems, 'e ran off into the desert.'

'What 'appened to 'im?'

'I don't know, but I heard a group of men from the dig went out looking for him. They came back at dusk. Couldn't find 'im anywhere.'

'Stupid boy. I seem to remember when he was a kid he was always doing something daft. I wonder what possessed him to go into the cave? Everybody knows aborigines are up there and it's not safe.'

'Hello Mrs Jones. You here again?' Stella interrupted.

'Yes dear—just wanted some more of that cream for my back. Really good it is,' she said. Smiling happily she turned back to her friend, but before she could say anything, Stella stepped between them.

'I hope you don't mind, but I couldn't help hearing you talking about somebody who'd been into a cave. Could it have been this cave?' she asked drawing her father's map from her pocket.

'I really don't know luv,' the woman replied peering at the map. 'I only heard about it from my John when he came home last night.'

'Oh well thanks anyway,' Stella replied. Disappointed, she put the map back in her pocket. 'It's your turn next,' she said politely and turned back to rolling bandages.

CHAPTER TWENTY-NINE

The sun was high in the sky—the heat relentless. Billy shaded his eyes with his hat and urged the bullocks forward. 'Do you think this is the right way?' he asked Zach who was sitting alongside him.

'Wallujabi said we should go this way, so this is the way we'll go,' Zach replied curtly, pulling his hat over his face, crossing his boots on the board in front of him.

'I don't like travelling in this heat and it sure ain't good for the bullocks,' Billy muttered under his breath. 'I can hardly see the track, the dust's almost covered it,' he whined, wiping his sweaty face with his hand. 'And we've got to find water soon or the bullocks will die on us.'

'Quit moaning Billy,' Zach said shortly. 'Wallujabi said to travel down this track until we came to the rocks. That's where we'd see the cave.' Pulling at a piece of rope tying a tin mug to a water bucket hanging on the side of the wagon, he half filled the mug and took a long drag of lukewarm water. Spitting to clear his mouth, he said, 'Have faith Billy,' and grabbing the reins from Billy's hands slashed the backs of the bullocks, driving them on until their breath came in long hard gasps and foam floated from their mouths. Angry, Billy tried to snatch the reins back, but the more he fought the more Zach laughed. It was not long before Zorro, exhausted and broken, dropped to his knees. The other bullocks, unable to stop, trampled him under their feet.

'Now look what you've done, Zach. How many times have you told me to be careful—that without the bullocks, we'll die,' Billy shouted and grabbing the water bucket from the side of the wagon, ran over to Zorro. Gently he lifted the bullock's head. 'There boy, take a drink,' he said, but Zorro just gazed up at him with sorrowful eyes. 'Don't give up now, we'll soon be at a waterhole,' Billy pleaded, holding out the bucket again.

'Out of my way, Billy. We've got three others bullocks and we can't waste time on this one,' Zach said, dragging a rifle from under the seat.

'No . . . I won't let you,' Billy's screamed, but as he struggled to get the gun out of Zach's hands, a shot echoed across the empty land. 'Now get these other animals under control so we can move on,' Zach shouted angrily.

Bitterness filled Billy's heart. When Zach disappeared into the wagon, he leaned over Zorro's dead body and let the tears flow.

CHAPTER THIRTY

The clinic had finished and Stella was sitting on her favourite rock at the edge of the campsite stroking Jacko's neck when a soft noise made her spring up. Without thinking she stuck out her hands defensively. 'Oh, Ah Fong, it's you. Don't you know, it's dangerous to creep up like that—I could've injured you.'

Ah Fong laughed. 'It is good that you able to defend yourself Stella,' he said pretending to return the attack.

Stella laughed back. 'Actually I'm glad you've come Ah Fong because I wanted to ask you something.'

'You did?'

'Yes. Whilst I was at the clinic today, I heard two women talking about a young lad who'd gone out to a cave at an Aborigine site.'

'And?'

'Well, they said he went into a cave and when he came out he'd gone mad.'

'How they know that?'

'I'm not sure, but that's what the woman said. I was only interested because I thought the cave might be the one my father wrote about. What do you think?' she asked, pulling her father's map from her pocket and spreading it out on the rock.

Ah Fong glanced at the paper then looked at Stella. 'I not the one you should be asking Stella. I think your friend Dhakhan more likely help you,' he answered looking thoughtfully at the sky as if expecting Dhakhan to appear out of nowhere.

'Do you think that was why Dhakhan brought me out here?' She was about to add something when Jacko ran down her arm, his ruff bright red. Eyes wide, she stared at him. Once he was sure he had her attention, he shot back up her arm and hid behind her neck.

'What was all that about Jacko? Were you trying to warn me of something?' she murmured, craning her neck to see where he was. But Jacko was already asleep and his ruff had returned to its normal blue/grey. Had he been trying to warn her? If he had, it must have been something to do with the cave, but what it was, she had no idea.

CHAPTER THIRTY-ONE

Stella was sitting beside the open tent flap tidying Hua's medicine box, when she saw Ranger Jack Thomas strolling through the line of tents.

'Good afternoon Sergeant,' she said, smiling into the Ranger's steely grey eyes. 'And what brings you here?'

'Two things, Miss Stella. First, I hear there are some nasty rumours being spread around the prospecting area up river.'

'Yes,' she replied. Unable to look at him, she stared down at her hands. 'Do you know anything about it?'

Stella shook her head. 'All I know is people are saying some gold has gone missing. The gossips have suggested Wang might have taken it. But he wouldn't do anything like that, I know he wouldn't,' she cried.

Sergeant Thomas looked down on her golden head, nodded, then stroked his chin. 'Australians don't like the Chinese because their ways are different. For some reason they're afraid they'll take over the country, but I think we've more to fear from the Japanese. They're the ones building up their armies.'

Stella nodded. 'Yes, I've heard that too.'

'Well that's as maybe,' he said, changing the subject. 'But there's another reason I needed to see you, Miss Stella. When I got back to Darwin, I made some enquiries about your ma,' he said, placing his large hand gently on her shoulder. 'And I'm sorry I'm the one who has to tell you this, but your ma's dead. It seems she died when the cyclone hit. My men called at your house to tell you or your brother, but there wasn't anybody there. My men reported that your brother Billy had left in the company of some gambling friends and you couldn't be found.'

'You mean Billy ran away?'

'It certainly looks like it. We're keeping an eye open for him and I'll let you know if we hear anything,' he said and, seeing the pain in her eyes, touched his hat and strode away.

Stella stared at the Ranger's retreating figure. Ma dead. A hand squeezed her heart, tears spilled down her cheeks leaving dirty patches as they dried. Silently she grieved for her mother. Memories of the day she'd heard her father had died came flooding back. She'd cried that day too, but not for long. Ma had put her arm around her shoulders and said, 'Tears don't get you through things Stella luv. It's a hard world and you got to show you got spirit.' Staring at the tents around her, she brushed the tears from her eyes. With both parents dead, her plans to return to Darwin seemed useless. But what about Billy? What was he was doing? Was he with his gambling friends? And did he know about ma? If he did, where was he? She looked down at Jacko licking the salty tears that had fallen on her arm. 'At least I've got you, Jacko,' she said, with a weak smile. Then she remembered she'd still got her pa's strike map. Knowing Billy as she did, she was sure he would look for the gold. So, if she could find out where the cave was, she might find Billy as well. With a heavy heart, she set her jaw, gathered up the bandages and went to tell Hua the sad news.

CHAPTER THIRTY-TWO

Billy yawned, watched the night turn to day. Poor Zorro, he didn't deserve to die. Without water he just couldn't keep up the brutal pace. Zach was the cruel one. He was lucky the three female bullocks had kept going. Suddenly his mourning was forgotten. Pulling the bullocks to a halt, he stared open mouthed at the huge rock rearing out of the early morning mist like a giant mammoth. Overwhelmed by its size, he watched the sun striking the layers of rock, turning them different shades of red. Suddenly he became aware of a dark opening between two of the layers. Like a giant's mouth, it beckoned, as if waiting to swallow anything that entered. Dark against the sun's rays, the cave sent out a threatening message.

'Zach, come and look at this,' he called, unwilling to go any closer.

Hearing the urgency in Billy's voice, Zach peeped out of the wagon. 'Well, what d'you know,' he drawled, his eyes dwelling on the cave's dark entrance. 'Looks like we might've found your pa's cave Billy lad.'

'Y . . . e . . . s. I seem to remember the drawing was something like this,' Billy replied. He looked over his shoulder at Zach's greedy eyes flicking over the rock. Unexplained fear rushed through him. Disgusted, he turned away. It was then his gaze fell on three gums growing beside the rock. The middle gum had been split by lightning. It was shedding droplets of moisture onto its curling bark and, in the strange light, Billy thought it looked like blood. Another worm of fear wriggled. These must be the trees his father had talked about, the ones he'd said would tell Billy he'd reached the strike. But was the blood an omen? Although the day was already hot, he shivered. The sound of the bullocks bellowing brought his thoughts back just in time to see Zach raise his whip. 'Zach,' he shouted. 'You'll kill Bessie like you killed Zorro, if you carry on like that. Then what'll we do?'

Zach, carried away by the thought of gold, let his arm fall. The whip cracked. Bessie gave one loud holler and shot forward, dragging Daisy and Patch with her. But she didn't run towards the rock. Instead she charged towards a small pool being fed from a waterfall trickling down the side of the rock. Unable to control the bullocks, Zach dropped the reins and jumped from the wagon. Running towards the cave, he shouted, 'Come on Ned. Let's go and find ol' man Tom's strike.'

Hearing the excitement in Zach's voice, Ned quickly joined him. Together, they ran to the cave's opening. Giggling, they vanished inside.' A minute later, they reappeared. 'Can't see a thing in there, Billy. Hand me a lantern,' Zach demanded.

Billy passed the lantern to Zach and watched them disappear back into the cave. He was just about to follow when he saw Wallujabi slithering towards him.

'Hello Wallujabi, what do you want?' he sighed, holding Bessie in check whilst she drank.

Wallujabi didn't reply. Instead, he shot into the air landing with a thump on Bessie's back, twisting its long body around the yoke across her shoulders. Terrified, she reared her head and bellowed.

'Whoa there Bessie,' Billy cried, clambering on board, hauling on the reins.

But Bessie was only aware of the snake tightening its grip. Hollering, she shot forward and dragging Daisy, Patch and the wagon with her, raced back into the desert.

CHAPTER THIRTY-THREE

Zach lit the lantern, squared his shoulders and stepped forward into the gloom of the cave.

'The gold's here, somewhere, I jus' know it,' he muttered. Ignoring the strange smell that closed in around him, he held the lantern high and made his way slowly down the tunnel.

It was not long before the air dried up and he began to gasp. When he came to a dry low ceilinged area, he stopped to get his breath. Light from the lantern fell along the walls. Peering forward, he gave a long low whistle. The walls were covered with pictures of red kangaroos jumping over dry cracked earth, snakes curling around trees and rain splashing on rocks. But it was the paintings of the Aborigines with their white painted faces and bodies that made goose pimples stand out on his arms. Sweating in the dry atmosphere, he wiped his brow, tried to go back, but his legs wouldn't move. Wondering where Ned was, he tried to call out, but all he could manage was a croak. Suddenly, the sticklike figures began to move. A didgeridoo began to play. One man looked at Zach, stepped down from the wall and walked slowly towards him.

The walls closed in. 'No . . . st . . . stay away from me,' Zach gasped. 'All I want is the gold.'

Other men stepped from the wall.

'No, go away,' Zach cried, shielding his face with his arm.

'You kill our brothers and sisters,' the leader said in a sing-song voice. 'Soon you go to your own Dreamtime.'

Drawing closer, they circled around him, pointing their spears at his chest.

Terrified, Zach crouched on the ground, tried to protect himself. 'I've done nothing to hurt you and I don't know anything about your brothers and sisters,' he shrieked staring wide eyed at their whitened hair and dusty grey bodies. The leader stepped forwards. In one hand he held a whip, in the other a skull. 'You white fella, you kill my tribe—pow.'

Helpless, Zach shrank away. 'I don't know anything about your tribe,' he howled. 'And I don't know anything about any killing. It must have been somebody else,' he cried, holding his hands over his ears, trying to shut out the sounds.

'You kill my people,' the leader insisted pounding the dusty cave floor with his bare feet.

'B . . . but . . . it wasn't me,' Zach said, beginning to blubber.

The stickmen, faces glowing eerily in the half light, opened their thick whitened lips and laughed. 'Man not strong—cry like baby,' the leader taunted, pricking Zach with his spear. Slowly they pressed closer, their eyes drawing him into their world. The leader, spear held high, drew closer and closer. The others followed.

Terrified, Zach's knees gave way and he slid to the cave floor. His head throbbed. The stale smell, coming from every corner of the cave, made him feel sick. Every time he tried to stand up, the leader leaned forward and pricked him with his spear. Blood dripped on to the cave floor. Desperate, Zach buried his head in his hands, tried to think of something that would make them go away. With one last defiant stand, he grabbed the lantern off the floor and held it over his head. 'I haven't come to kill your people. All I want is the gold,' he repeated, eyes fixed on their leader.

In the lantern light, alarm appeared in the men's eyes.

They began to fade.

Quickly, Zach turned up the wick, held the lantern out in front of him. Dazzled by the bright light they stopped chanting and backed away. Slowly, one by one, they slid back onto the wall of the cave.

Shaken by what had happened, Zach waited, but the men didn't move. Feeling more confident, he held the lantern close to the wall and noticed a sparkling river winding its way across the landscape. He peered closer. In the half light, he saw it was not a river, but a seam of gold running through the wall and the stick-like figures were kneeling beside it!

'Tis the gold,' he whispered, running his fingers along the seam, shivering in excitement. A sound from the tunnel made him look round. 'Thank goodness, it's you Ned. Where've you been?' he exclaimed. 'Come and look at this.'

'What is it Zach?' Ned asked, stumbling into the cave.

'I'm not sure. A moment ago I thought they were just paintings, but when I looked closer I saw . . .' He stopped and pointed a shaking finger at the golden river.

Ned giggled. 'Is it gold Zach?' he asked excitedly, moving a step closer.

There was a rustle on the cave floor.

'I think so,' Zach continued, eagerly tracing his fingers across the golden river. 'Come and . . .' He looked over his shoulder and his eyes filled with horror. A black python, eyes glittering in the half light, was swallowing Ned's arm. Terrified, he looked around for a stick or something he could use to hit the snake, but the snake held his eyes and he couldn't move.

'Za . . . ch, he . . . lp,' Ned gasped, but Zach was under the snake's hypnotic gaze. All he could do was watch as the snake wrapped its coils around Ned's body, squeezing him until he could no longer breathe.

Eventually the snake's power began to fade and Zach was released from its hypnotic gaze. The snake raised its head, prepared to strike again, but it was weary. The struggle with Ned had taken its energy and it could only move slowly. Crazy with fear, Zach stumbled down the tunnel, back to the cave's entrance. Gasping with relief, when he saw the snake hadn't followed, he looked around for Billy.

'Billy, where are you?' he called, expecting to see the wagon and the bullocks waiting for him. 'Billy?' he called again . . . and again. When finally he realised Billy was not there and the wagon had gone, he slumped against a tree, wiped the perspiration from his face. 'He'll be back shortly,' he growled angrily, staring at the dry earth. He settled down to wait, but his nerves were on edge. Restless, his eyes flicked here and there. When he saw the python slithering towards him again, he let out a long piercing scream and scrambled to his feet. Desperate to get away, not bothering to look where he was going, he ran into the desert. In the merciless heat it was not long before he was exhausted. Defeated, he fell to the ground. The sun beat down on his body.

CHAPTER THIRTY-FOUR

The early morning sun, alive with heat, crept over the horizon. Knee deep in the river, Wang's eyes hunted through the water to the riverbed where he knew the gold would be. He'd heard others shouting when they had found such a rock, but so far he'd not had this luck. Strangely, he was not unhappy. Hua had her clinic and Ah Fong would soon be a man. Always up at daybreak, he liked to search the riverbed before the water became cloudy with silt from upstream. Thrusting his fist into the water, he drew out a piece of rock. His heart began to pound in his ears. 'Gold,' he shouted at the top of his voice, holding his hand high in the air as he'd seen the others do. Breathing hard he opened his hand and squinted at the gold flecks in the pebble. His throat tightened with excitement. Suddenly he felt afraid and closed his hand, but every prospector in the river had heard him shout and were wading towards him. Wang straightened his back and waited. The men closed in. He saw the greed written on their faces. Long cotton trousers clinging to his legs, he tried to break through the ring of men, but he was knee deep in water and the wet trousers held him back. The crowd thickened. His fear increased. From behind, fingers fastened on his shoulders, pushed him down. He tried to pull free, but the fingers were strong and he fell backwards. As he fell he opened his mouth, 'Ah Fong,' he spluttered as he went under. Up, down, up down, again and again his head disappeared beneath the water. Memories of his homeland swirled in his mind. He saw Hua, his wife. She was smiling at him and Stella, the lonely Australian girl was trying to say something. Gradually their faces disappeared and he drifted towards the bright light that beckoned him.

CHAPTER THIRTY-FIVE

Stella noticed the line of patients melting away. She could hear shouting—it was coming from the river. Something was wrong.

'There's been a find,' a fat woman cried, shoving Stella to one side, running with her skirts high over her knees.

'You mean gold?' Stella panted, keeping pace with her.

'Yes dearie, that's what all this noise usually means. Hope it's my Joe,' she said pushing through the crowds that were already lining the banks of the river.

Stella followed. When she got to the water's edge, she saw upstream, a group of men holding a man by his hair; saw a pigtail fly in the air. Immediately she knew it must be Wang. Fear for his safety gripped her. 'Wang,' she cried, pushing and splashing through the water, trying to get to him, but every prospector seemed to be in the water blocking her way.

'One, two, three.' Stella's heart sank—Wang was getting a dunking. Standing on tip-toe, she tried to look over the top of the crowd, but it was impossible to see anything. Quickly she realised she wouldn't be able to get to Wang and fled from the river back to the tent.

'Hua, come quickly,' she shouted, pulling back the flap. 'It's Wang. They're dunking him in the river. Where's Ah Fong? Wang needs him' she cried.

'Ah Fong not here, Stella. He go find koala bear. We go help Wang,' she said, and pulling on her pointed Chinese hat trotted towards the river.

Stella looked at Hua's bent back disappearing into the crowds. It only took a second for her to change her mind. Forgetting Ah Fong, she pushed and shoved through the crowd until she was back at the water's edge again. Wang was lying face down in the water and Hua was bending over him. 'Excuse me. Please let me through,' she sobbed, jostling the crowd with her elbows. When the women saw who it was, they stepped aside to let her through. Together, she and Hua lifted Wang's body out of the river. He was unconscious, his face drawn and shrivelled, his hands clenched. Water leaked from every corner of his jacket and trousers. Shocked by what had happened, Stella turned to the prospectors for help, but the hard look in their eyes told her they weren't going to make things easy.

'I'm going to tell the Rangers about this,' she shouted, angry with herself for not going Wang's aid when she'd first heard the shouting, but as quickly as her anger had started, it disappeared. 'You,' she shouted at three men who had worked next to Wang and knew him well. 'Don't just stand there. Please help me take him back to their tent.' Humiliated by her words, the three prospectors moved forwards, took Wang in their arms and carried him away from the river.

'Well, don't just leave him there,' Stella snapped when they propped Wang's body against the side of the tent. 'Take him inside. Can't you see he's dying?'

Ashamed, they picked him up and carried him into the tent where they gently laid him on the makeshift bed.

'I'll get the priest,' one of the men said.

'Don't bother, he's Chinee,' someone answered.

Hua raised her eyes to the crowd. 'Leave us,' she said, her quiet voice full of grief. 'Wang kind man, he hurt nobody. Now, please go . . . .' Without another word she bent over Wang's still body and began to weep.

CHAPTER THIRTY-SIX

Ah Fong was climbing to the top branch of a gum tree, reaching out to a furry koala bear, when he heard the shouting. It was normally quiet at that time of the morning and he knew something must be wrong. He looked across the dry scrub to where the tents were pitched. Leaning further out to get a better view, he didn't notice the branch bending, nor see the bark peeling from under his foot. Suddenly his thin slipper lost its grip and he was falling. He grabbed at some leaves. They came away in his hand. The hard earth raced towards him. Suddenly strong arms closed around him and he was rushing back into the tree. Laughter made him open his eyes. He blinked and stared at the young Aborigine boy sitting on the branch beside him.

'I am Dharkan,' the boy said. 'Wang, your father, need help. Your mother good to Stella of the Skies,—now I help you,' he said simply and before Ah Fong could reply, he had grabbed him round the waist and they were flying out of the tree back to his tent. There, Dhakhan set him down. Ah Fong bowed to Dhakhan, smiled his thanks and turned to Stella who was standing by the tent flap.

'Wh . . . what . . . they do to my father?' he asked, his voice shaky.

'Where've you been Ah Fong? Stella asked, ignoring his question, anger bubbling through her words. 'You should've been here—your father needed you. I hope you're not too late,' she said, her voice softening when she saw the hurt in his eyes.

Ah Fong stepped inside the tent. When he saw his father's pale face, he fell to his knees. After a while he took the corner of his father's tunic and dried the drops of water that still ran down his wrinkled neck.

Suddenly Wang opened his eyes. Seeing Ah Fong, his eyes filled with happiness. 'I find gold Ah Fong,' he whispered proudly, opening his fist to show Ah Fong the rock he'd somehow managed to hide. When he looked at his son again, his blue lips turned up in a half smile. 'You good boy Ah Fong,' he said softly, voice weakening. 'You head of family now. You look after my Hua for me.' Hearing the rustle of wings on his shoulder, he placed the rock in Ah Fong's hand and whispered—'Gold make you rich Ah Fong.'

Numb, Ah Fong held his hand. When he heard Hua's long wail he knew his father had left this world.

CHAPTER THIRTY-SEVEN

Heads deep in a news sheet, two women whispered. Something about their manner made Stella curious. Craning her head over their bent shoulders, she read the headline. 'Death by Misadventure.' Furious, she didn't stop to read any more and hurried back to the tent where Hua was finishing her daily clinic. 'Hua,' she called. 'I've just seen the news sheet. The Coroner's verdict was Death by Misadventure.' Grim-faced, she saw the shock on Hua's face. 'I guess they all stuck to the same story and what really happened will probably never be told,' she said, straightening her shoulders. 'So what are we going to do Hua?'

Eyes filled with sadness, Hua looked at her. 'Wang want to stay here, so we stay. Ah Fong look after us,' she said and turned away so Stella couldn't read what was in her eyes.

A few days later Stella walked by the river, deep in thought. Why had Hua turned away? Wouldn't even speak to her? Saddened by Hua's change, Stella would have liked to talk to Ah Fong about it, but he too was hard to find now. She understood their grief, but couldn't understand why they were ignoring her. Wang had always protected her, given her security, but now, without him, her future was uncertain. Holding her head high, she walked on, watched some stray dogs searching for scraps. There had to be something better than this, she thought, wrinkling her nose at the rats scuttling in the garbage. Still thinking about Ah Fong's long absences, she walked back to the tent. 'Hua, you there?' she called.

'Yes, Stella.,' Hua replied. 'What you want?'

'I need to speak to you.'

'Talk to Ah Fong,' Hua replied sharply. 'And Stella, please leave. I wish to be alone.'

Puzzled and hurt by Hua's sharp tone, Stella stepped back out of the tent. What had happened wasn't her fault. Squaring her shoulders, she decided to go and find Ah Fong—speak to him now. Determined, she marched out of the camp in the direction of the red boulders where Ah Fong spent so much of his time.

CHAPTER THIRTY-EIGHT

The three terrified bullocks fled across the parched land, running until they could run no more. Broken, they fell to their knees on a ridge of hard sand. Billy jumped off the wagon and ran to where they lay. 'Get up Bessie, get up,' he urged, easing the heavy yoke from around her neck. After a while she got to her feet. Billy had just turned his attention to Daisy and Patch when she gave another holler and took off. Knocking Billy off his feet, she dragged the wagon and her two companions along the ridge of sand.

'Bessie,' Billy screamed as the wagon teetered on the edge of the ridge. Too far away to do anything, he could only watch as, metal clanging on metal, the wagon tumbled down the side of the gulley, careered along the bottom of the dry gulley and crashed against a large boulder. Shocked, Billy, looked down at the twisted wagon. But his main thought was for the bullocks. Were they still alive? As he scrambled down the side of the valley, narrowing his eyes against the sun's glare, he could just see them lying in a heap beside the wagon. Praying they were still alive, he ran towards them. When he got there, he flung himself beside Bessie. Sick at heart, he stroked her head and whispered her name. Hearing his voice, she pricked one ear and looked at him with soulful eyes. He stroked her, the way he'd done so many times before, but she didn't move. He turned to look at Daisy and Patch. They were lying beside each other, eyes closed. The sun blazed down. Fear struck him again—this time hard and fierce. He had to find water.

He looked down the valley. A short distance away, two hillocks had split in two. Wondering what was on the other side, he ran towards them. Breathing heavily, but determined to get to the other side of the valley, he pushed his body into the narrow gap. Scratching his hands on the sides, he scrabbled and pushed his way through. A few minutes later, he burst through to the other side and let out a shout of joy. Only fifty yards away was an inland lake and bedside it shady gums and palms swayed gently in the soft breeze. Limping to the water's edge, he flung himself down and drank until he couldn't drink any more. Then he remembered the bullocks. Ashamed he hadn't thought of them first, he returned to the wagon, found a sturdy bucket and stumbled back to the lake. There, he filled the bucket and carried it carefully back to the bullocks. Smelling water, they snorted quietly and lifted their heads. Taking Bessie's head in his hands, he held the bucket so she could drink. Then he did the same thing for Patch and Daisy. Six times he returned to the lake to fill the bucket. Eventually, Bessie got to her feet—Patch and Daisy followed her. Carefully, Billy led the three bullocks to the end of the valley, round the last hill and back down to the water. There he patiently waited until they had had enough to drink then tethered them under a shady tree. Overcome by the intense heat, mixed with relief the bullocks were all right, Billy staggered to the nearest shady rock and slithered down to the soft sandy soil. For the first time that day he closed his eyes.

CHAPTER THIRTY-NINE

Stella picked her way across the dry scrub to the round boulders where she found Ah Fong standing on one of the rocks. Cupping her hands round her mouth, she called, 'Ah Fong, please come down. I want to talk to you.'

Ah Fong turned towards her. 'What you want?' he shouted back. 'Your people not want us. I am head of family now. Better I take my mother to homeland.'

'No Ah Fong. Your father wanted you to build a life here in Australia. And please come down, I can't talk to you up there.'

'I not want to come there,'

'You must, Ah Fong. You can't stay up there forever and Hua needs you,' she pleaded. Then, making up her mind to wait until he did come down, she settled Jacko around her neck, leaned her head against the rock's smooth side and stared at the barren landscape.

A soft noise made her look round—Ah Fong was standing a short distance from where she sat.

'Come and sit here,' she said, patting the rock.

Shrugging his shoulders, Ah Fong sat down.

'I understand your pain Ah Fong. My ma died in the cyclone in Darwin, remember? We can't pretend Wang is still here. He's not and we've got to talk about what we should do.'

Ah Fong shook his head sadly. 'Your people not like us, Stella. I wish to go back to my homeland, but my mother she want what my father Wang want to make new home in this country. Maybe we stay here.'

'You sure?' she asked.

'Yes,' he said, nodding. 'I not tell you, Stella, because I want to go back to my homeland. My mother say Wang brought us here because he afraid of war in our country and because this is what she want, we stay.'

Stella nodded. 'Your mother is wise medicine woman. She will follow Wang's wishes.'

Ah Fong nodded and stood up. 'Yes, Stella,' he said, bowing low.

Stella bowed back and watched him disappear as silently as he had arrived. She still didn't understand why he had become so distant.

Jacko ran down her arm onto her wrist. She sighed and scratched his head. Not wanting to go back to the camp, she sat in the shady hollow and stared at the bare landscape. It was not long before her mind began to wander. 'Dhakhan, Dhakhan, Dhakhan,' she whispered, the words slipping from her lips.

'You called Stella of the Skies?'

Startled, she squinted into the sunlight and saw Dhakhan standing on top of the boulder, smiling down at her.

'Dhakhan, you've come,' she whispered softly.

'Yes, Stella of the Skies, I come. Why do you call?'

'Dhakhan, I feel so alone. Ma's dead and I don't know where Billy is. Now my friend Wang is dead and Hua and Ah Fong don't need me, I don't know what to do,' she said, choking back her tears. 'Ah Fong says he wants to take his mother back to their homeland. Oh Dharkan, I'm so lonely,' she blurted, forbidden tears trickling down her cheeks.

Dhakhan shook his head sadly. 'Stella, do not be unhappy. Go to Alice Springs. There you will find happiness.'

'Alice Springs—why there?'

Dhakhan smiled down on her. 'Your destiny Stella,' he said softly.

Stella lifted her head to ask what he meant, but he was already fading and she was left staring at the empty rock. Why did he always disappear just when she wanted to know more, she thought? But his words had given her fresh courage. Straightening her shoulders, she stood up. Head high, she shielded her eyes against the sun and looked towards the south. Alice Springs was another 350 miles further down the track—a long way to travel on her own. Then her eyes slid to the long line of tents shimmering in the heat. She was tired of living in a tent. There had to be something better than that. With a heavy heart, she made her decision. She would go to Alice. What she would do when she got there, she had no idea.

CHAPTER FORTY

The sun blazed down on Billy's head. Stunned, he rubbed his sore eyes, licked his salty parched lips. A moment later the horror of what had happened swept through him. He sat up with a jolt and breathed a sigh of relief when he saw the bullocks were still in the shade where he'd left them. Staggering over to them, he stroked and talked to them, ran his hands over their sides and down their legs. When he found they were OK, he scrambled over the dusty ground to the water and bathed, splashing water over his head, cooling his sore body. Lying in the water on the edge of the lake, he looked up at the sky. A bunch of dates hung in one of the palm trees. His stomach rumbled reminding him he hadn't eaten since the day before. Mouth watering, he put his arms around the tree and shook it. Nothing happened. Then he remembered seeing some Aborigine boys climbing trees. Copying them, he put his arms and legs around the trunk and dragged himself upwards. He quickly developed a gentle rocking movement and it was not long before he was underneath the dates. Reaching up, his fingers were just about to close around them, when suddenly they tore from the branch and fell to the ground. Annoyed, but thankful he had something to eat, he slid back down the tree and grabbed the dates. He was about to pop one in his mouth, when he saw a black head swinging from a branch above his head. It wasWallujabi!

'How did you get here Wallujabi and wh . . . what do you want?' he mumbled shoving the dates into his mouth.

'Wallujabi, Spirit of the Desert, go everywhere,' the snake said, uncurling his body, dropping to the ground. 'You safe Billy because, Wallujabi, take you from danger. Many die in cave, but you not die there.'

Before Billy could reply, he continued, 'You brother of Stella?'

'Yes, I . . . er . . . had a sister called Stella. Why do you ask?' Billy stared at the snake, wondering how he knew he had a sister.

Wallujabi drew his lips back and spoke softly. 'She live in Tennant Creek.'

'I don't believe you,' Billy cried. 'She . . . we . . . lived in Darwin and I was told she'd drowned in the floods.'

'She alive . . . in Tennant Creek,' the snake insisted. 'You go there.'

'W . . . ell . . . if you say so,' Billy said slyly, thinking it might be better not to argue. 'But first I must go back to the cave—find my friends—and my father's gold.'

'Your friends?' Wallujabi sneered. 'They not your friends Billy. They only cheat you.'

'But . . .' Billy stared at the snake, watched it coiling its body.

Wallujabi raised his head and stared at Billy through cold slanted eyes. 'Track show you way to Tennant Creek. Cave belong my ancestor, not white fella. You go to cave, you meet danger.'

Billy thought for a moment—Zach had said Stella was dead and the only reason he'd been persuaded to come into the desert was to find his pa's gold. 'Wallujabi, Spirit of the Desert,' he wheedled, 'You said you would take me to the cave where I would find my father's strike, so why have you brought me here?'

'You draw picture—say you want go that place—so I take you, but it cave of my people—their Dreaming place. White fella kill my people.' Wallujabi hissed angrily. 'You go there, you die like your friends,' he snapped.

'Die like my friends?' Billy stammered, looking for the snake, wondering where he'd gone.

Laughter echoed out from under a large stone. 'You must decide, Billy.'

Then there was silence.

Billy spent the rest of the day mending the wagon. Tired, he stared at the stone where the snake had disappeared. Could he believe what the snake said? He watched the first shades of night streak the sky. Night came quickly in the desert. Somewhere, out in the distance, a dingo howled. Fear tightened his stomach. Gathering some sticks and small branches, he dug a hole, placed a few stones around it and made a fire. When it was burning brightly, he pulled a blanket from the wagon and lay down. Comforted by the fire's warmth, he soon fell asleep. In his dreams he saw his father. 'Billy, lad,' his father said, 'Forget the gold. Go back before the greed gets you as it got me and Zach. Go back before it's too late,' he said sadly, shaking his head.

Billy woke with a start. The fire was almost out. Shivering in the cold night air, he poked the dying embers, got the fire going again and put on the billycan. With the dream still fresh in his mind, he huddled over the flames, sipped the hot sweet tea and gazed at the thousands of glittering stars. Had Wallujabi been telling the truth? Was Stella in Tennant Creek? It didn't make sense. No, he couldn't trust the snake. Throwing the remaining tea onto the fire to put out the flames, he climbed up to the seat in front of the wagon and stared at the brilliant sky. He thought about his ma and Stella and how poor they'd been. No, he wasn't going to be poor. He was going to be rich. He would go south and find his pa's gold!

CHAPTER FORTY-ONE

Billy travelled all night. Tired, but determined, he drove on until the stars disappeared and the sun was peeping over the horizon. A sudden movement in the haze ahead made him sit up, pay attention. Gradually the dust took shape. Two horsemen were coming towards him. Squinting in the hard morning light, he pulled the wagon to a halt.

'G-day,' he drawled to the two men as they drew alongside.

'G-day to you young man,' the older man said, his manner friendly and warm.

'Where're you headed?'

'I'm not sure,' Billy answered. 'I was goin' to this place,' he said pulling the drawing of his pa's map from his pocket.

The older man took it and frowned. 'This place is on Aborigine land,' he said.

'It is?' Billy queried, remembering Wallujabi's warning.

'Yeah, it sure is an' they'll kill you if they find you there. You on your own?'

Billy looked the man square in the eyes. 'Yes, and as I told you, I'm looking for my pa's gold strike.'

The man looked back at Billy, studied him long and hard. 'You're a bit young to be out here on your own aren't you? The outback's a hard place and if you go here,' he said jabbing a finger at the map, 'it could be the last thing you ever do.' Slowly he handed the map back, looking at Billy for a long time. At last, he said, 'If its good honest work you're looking for, we could do with an extra hand at the Lazy S station. This is cattle country round here boy, you any good with animals?'

Billy nodded. 'Yeah, I've looked after my bullocks well enough, Mr er . . .'

'Just call me boss,' the man replied, his eyes resting on the bullocks feeding quietly on the tough grass beside the track. 'I'm the owner of the Lazy S cattle station over there,' he added waving his arm in the general direction of the land to the east. 'I run about 20,000 head of cattle. Jake, my leading stockman's gettin' old and I'm looking for another man to train up. So, if you're a hard worker and want to come back with us, my missus'll give you a good breakfast. You can take a look around, see what you think.'

'Thanks, I think I might do that' Billy replied, grinning broadly at the prospect of a hearty breakfast. Touching his hat, he flicked the reins gently, called to Bessie and followed the two horsemen back to the Lazy S cattle station.

CHAPTER FORTY-TWO

Stella packed her things, said good-bye to Hua and Ah Fong, and joined the crowd outside the saloon where the coach waited. Nervous, she watched the passengers climb onto the open topped coach. She could still change her mind, she thought, looking over her shoulder hoping to see either Ah Fong or Hua trotting towards her, but there was nobody in sight. Hurt by their rejection, she pushed thoughts of what she would do when she got to Alice Springs out of her mind, picked up the skin bag containing her few belongings and clambered up the steps of the coach.

'This is not enough,' the coach driver said, looking at the few pence she placed in his hand.

'But that's all I've got,' Stella replied quickly. Suddenly afraid he was going to turn her away, she said. 'Please Mister, I've got to get to Alice. I don't have to sit in the coach, I can sit beside you. Please,' she begged, her golden eyes pleading. 'I'll pay the rest when I get work, honest I will,' she rushed on.

The driver looked down at the tousled girl and shook his head. 'No, I can't do that.'

'Why not?' Stella demanded, anger burning her cheeks.

The driver looked at her again. She might be genuine, he thought, thinking of his own daughter. 'Where's your ma and why's it so important you go to Alice?' he asked.

'My ma's dead—drowned in the Darwin cyclone,' she replied, lowering her eyes. 'Please, please take me to Alice. I . . . I want to be a . . . a flying doctor,' she said, blurting out the first thing she could think of.

'Do you now?' the driver replied, a small smile edging the corners of his mouth. Suddenly he relented. 'OK sit up here, but don't get in the way. The horses can be troublesome if they know there are strangers up here.'

'Thanks Mister. I appreciate your kindness,' Stella replied politely. 'How long does it take to get to Alice?' she asked, jumping up, sitting beside him.

'Oh, not long, 'bout five days.'

'Five days?' Stella exclaimed, 'th . . . that long?'

He laughed. 'Well, it's about 350 miles. We stop overnight, get some rest, then set off the following morning. We'll be down in Alice for breakfast on Friday,' he said, looking at her long and hard. Then, making up his mind she was none of his business, flicked the horse's reins. The coach wheels spun, the horses gathered speed and they were off down the hard track that led to Alice Springs.

Five days later, stiff and tired from spending sleepless nights on hotel verandahs and hours sitting on the bench beside the coach driver, Stella stepped wearily onto the dusty main street in Alice Springs.

'Thanks Mister, I promise I'll get the money for my fare, pay you back—you just see,' she said, smiling up at him.

The coach driver looked down at the girl. 'Mrs Jones at No 10 takes in lodgers. She might be able to help you,' he said. 'And if you're in any kind of trouble, go in there and ask for Annie,' he added nodding his head in the direction of the saloon. 'She knows everything that goes on in Alice,' he said, and flicking the reins, guided the coach and horses towards the stables.

'Thanks for your kindness' Stella called after him, voice trailing off. She looked up and down the street, not sure what to do. Then she reminded herself she'd come to Alice to start a new life, so she squared her shoulders, picked up her bag and trudged down the dusty street.

CHAPTER FORTY-THREE

Hot under the blazing sun, Stella walked slowly down the only street in Alice. When she came to a bench on the shady board walk, she slumped down. Wiping her hot face, she admired the yellow spurs of the wattles growing in the middle of the street. It was Springtime and the yellow blossom made her feel hopeful. She was wondering what she should do next when she spotted a flag fluttering on a building at the end of the street. It was too early to look for lodgings so she decided to stroll down and have a look. The building was set back from the street, and its double doors and fluted columns gave it an old fashioned look. However, it was the sign above the door—FLYING DOCTOR SERVICE—that held her attention. Underneath she read ALICE SPRINGS CONTROL STATION. Her heart began to thump. Above the door, a map of Australia with wings on either side, gave the building a feeling of authority. She wondered if she dared go inside, but decided against it. Taking her time, she walked round the back of the building. Her heart gave another leap. At the end of a short runway, two bi-planes with the words 'Flying Doctor Service' written on their sides, were preparing to take off. Wanting to see more, she strode over to the nearest plane and was standing at the foot of the steps imagining what it was like in the cockpit, when a voice from behind made her jump.

'And what d'you think you're doing?'

Flustered, Stella spun round and found she was looking into the bluest eyes of the most handsome man she'd ever seen. Wearing dark blue shorts and long white socks, his muscular tanned body glowed with health. 'Well?' he asked again.

'I . . . I was just looking at the plane,' she stuttered, not knowing what else to say.

'Were you now,' he mocked. 'And I suppose you're going to tell me you want to be a Flying Doctor.'

Stella nodded, 'How did you know that?'

'They all do,' the man replied. 'Come along now, off you go. It's dangerous playing about near the planes.'

'I'm not playing about—I'm serious,' Stella replied crossly.

'How old are you?'

'I'm coming up fourteen,' she replied, stretching the truth a little.

'Well you don't suddenly become a Flying Doctor, you know. You have to train first and sometimes even learn to fly one of these,' he said, patting the plane's nose cone. 'I'm Dr Bennett by the way,' he said, holding out his hand.

'Nice to meet you Dr Bennett,' Stella replied, shaking his hand. 'Well, if you're already a Flying Doctor, you can tell me what I have to do—you know—how I become one—like you,' she said boldly. 'I could help in your office, or something like that,' she rushed on determined not to let the opportunity slip away.

'Well, you'd have to start at the bottom and work hard,' he said, looking into her eager face, seeking something that would tell him she really was serious. After a while, he said, 'If you really are serious, come and see me at the clinic here on Tuesday, 08.00 sharp. The sisters from the hospital usually come over then and I'm sure they could do with some help. We'll take the rest as it comes, OK?'

'Uh, will I get paid? You see I don't have any money and I already owe the coach driver for my fare.'

Dr Bennett laughed. 'That depends on you, young lady. Where's your ma and pa?'

'They're dead, killed in the cyclone,' she said, blushing at the half truth. 'I've gotta look after myself now and I need a job, a regular job.'

Dr Bennett looked at the blonde girl standing in front of him—saw the grave expression on her face. 'Well, if you do what you're told, we might be able to come to some arrangement. I'm not promising though, you've got to prove you're reliable first,' he said, walking towards a door in the back of the building marked 'Office.'

'Thanks Dr Bennett. I won't let you down, I promise,' she called after him. Unable to believe her luck, she half-ran, half-skipped back down the street to find lodgings.

CHAPTER FORTY-FOUR

Billy walked from the shed towards the lean-to where the other stockmen were already waiting for breakfast. The smell of breakfast steak, damper and tea made his stomach growl.

Since he had joined the Lazy S station six months ago, Billy had grown to over six feet and his arms were thick with muscles. He had worked hard and, apart from his usual jobs, he'd been given two baby calves to look after as well as his own three bullocks. He was on his way to feed them when a voice called out—

'Hey, Billy, the Boss wants you over at the Big House.'

Billy looked round and saw Al on the other side of the yard waving his arms. 'OK, what's he want?'

'I don' know, but you'd best be quick, he's not in a good mood today,' Al called back.

Putting thoughts of breakfast to one side, Billy strolled towards the Big House, wondering what the Boss could possibly want. He hadn't spoken to him since Billy's first day at the station. Since then, Billy had learned to ride a horse and lasso and tether a cow as efficiently as any man on the station. He loved the outdoor life and was proud of the fact that he had done well since he had joined the other cattlemen at the Lazy S. Nervous, he walked towards the door marked 'Office'.

'Come,' a voice called in answer to his knock. Slowly Billy eased the door open, took off his hat and stepped inside. Dark, compared to the bright sunlight outside, he peered at the man sitting behind the old fashioned desk in the corner.

'Come in, Billy,' the man called out. Pointing to a small table he said, 'Help yourself to some coffee and rest your legs awhile.'

Billy nodded. 'Thanks,' he replied, slowly walking towards the table. Pouring coffee into one of the tin mugs, he looked at the man they all called The Boss. His face was tanned to a dark brown and deeply lined. However, it was his searching eyes that impressed Billy and held his attention.

'You enjoy working at the Lazy S Billy?' Boss asked at last, running his eyes over Billy's sparse body and firm hands.

Billy nodded.

'You've been with us for six months now and Jake's told me how well you did at the mustering camp. Now I need to find out how good you are on your own. How d'you feel about taking a herd down to Alice and loading them on to the trucks there? Jake's a bit crook at the moment, so we'd like you to take the herd. Shorty and Japaljarri will be going with you, but I need you to be in charge as they're likely to go walkabouts once they get to Alice. I want you to make sure the herd gets on the train. It's a big responsibility Billy. Think you can do it?'

'Sure, Boss,' Billy replied eagerly. 'But why not Shorty or Japal? I've seen them rounding up the cows. They're good stockmen.'

'Yes they are Billy, but I'm looking for someone to take over from Jake and this is your opportunity to make your mark at the Lazy S, Come and see me in the morning and I'll give you your final instructions. Understood?'

'Yes sir,' Billy exclaimed, finding his voice at last. 'What time do we get started? Alice is about 50 miles from here, so how long does it take?'

'I reckon about two days. You can spend a day in Alice if you like. Shorty likes to go and see his invalid sister who lives there and it'll give you a chance to look around.

'Thanks Boss. I'd like that.'

'OK Billy, off you go. Make all your arrangements through Jake. That's all.'

Hardly able to believe his luck, Billy muttered a quick 'thank you' and rushed out the door.

The next morning, Billy woke early. He leapt from his bunk, watered and fed the bullocks and made sure Mary, the Aborigine girl who helped cook, knew exactly what to do with the calves. Then he strode towards the Big House. Excitement clipped his feet. Today he was going to take the herd to Alice, but more importantly Boss was putting him in charge. With the new responsibility whirling in his head, he headed towards the gate that separated the Big House from the rest of the station.

CHAPTER FORTY-FIVE

From the rock where he practised kung fu, Ah Fong watched the coach leave. Determined not to dwell on something he could do nothing about, he punched the air and kicked out at an imaginary challenger. Stella was free to do what she wanted. His mother needed him now his father had gone. With a whirl, he jumped down landing beside a rounded red rock he called the baby stone. Running his hands down its sides, he gently rolled it to one side and checked that the gold rock his father had pressed into his hand was still there. Satisfied it was safely hidden, he rolled the stone back into place and smoothed the sand around it. He knew the gold rock must be worth a lot of money or the other prospectors wouldn't have been interested. Somehow he would have to get it weighed, but he would have to be careful. He knew for certain now that the other prospectors would say he'd stolen it.

Every day since Stella had gone, Ah Fong had suggested to his mother they should go to Alice to get the gold rock weighed. Every day she'd said 'No.' He understood it was because his father had died in Tennant Creek that she wanted to stay, but he didn't like living there and was tired of living in a tent. When he went to the river, the other prospectors ignored him and he was afraid one day they would attack him or his mother. However, the gold wasn't the only reason he wanted to go to Alice. He missed Stella and wanted to see her again.

'Mama,' he said one day, squatting beside his mother who was washing the dishes after their evening meal. 'We must sell rock, find somewhere to live,' he insisted. 'You not strong now and Wang, my father, not wish us always to live in tent. We go to Alice, get rock weighed—buy a store. Perhaps you start new clinic there.'

Hua looked at her son for a long time. 'Yes, Ah Fong you right,' she said eventually. 'We go to Alice, get rock weighed. Now Stella not here, clinic not good. Tomorrow, we go,' she said and without discussing the matter further started to pack their few belongings.

Ah Fong drove the donkey down the centre of Alice Springs and tethered it in front of a sign that read Miners' Office. As he passed the small dirty window, he looked inside. Apart from the man leaning on the counter reading a news sheet, it was empty. Full of hope, he opened the door and walked in.

'How much this in money?' he asked, placing the rock on the counter.

The man stared at the rock for a long time, turning it over and over in his hands. 'This is good gold, Chinee. Where'd you get it?'

'My father find it—give to me.'

The man looked at him again. 'You tellin' the truth?'

'Yes, that true. I want buy store in Alice,' Ah Fong replied. 'Alice need good Emporium. How much you give for gold rock?'

The man looked at Ah Fong. You could never tell what the Chinee were thinking, he thought, but Alice certainly needed a good store and the Chinee were known to be hard workers. Picking up the rock, he placed it on the weighing machine. There were strict laws regarding gold registration, but he could make sure nobody knew about the rock. 'Fifteen guineas,' he said, putting the rock on the bench.

Ah Fong stared at the man, saw his greedy eyes slide sideways. The man was cheating him—but fifteen guineas—that was more than enough to buy a store and make him a wealthy man. He nodded in agreement. 'I take money now,' he said and taking out a drawstring bag he had tied around his waist, waited for the man to open his safe.

'Put your thumb mark there,' the man said, pointing at a black ink pad then at a piece of paper.

'That all?' Ah Fong asked.

The man nodded.

With the money safely hidden under his tunic, Ah Fong tore the 'for sale' notice off the post outside the Registry Office and walked towards the Royal Hotel. He didn't like saloons, but he knew it was the sort of place where he could find out how to purchase a store. He looked at the building on the poster. It would make a fine emporium. Pushing open the saloon doors, he walked up to the bar and held out the poster to the woman behind the bar.

'This emporium—It for sale?' he asked, waving the picture of the store in front of her. 'Where I go buy it?'

Annie stared at the young Chinese man standing in her bar. Chinese didn't come into The Royal. 'Well, that a fact?' she asked, smiling gently into Ah Fong's eager face. 'You got money?'

Ah Fong nodded. 'My father die and give gold rock to me,' he said, his voice strong and determined. 'I come to Alice to buy emporium. Ah Fong and Hua, my mother, work hard—make emporium good for people of Alice.'

'That so . . .' Annie said cautiously. She'd seen many men come into her saloon and was a good judge of character. She stared long and hard at Ah Fong. It didn't take her long to make up her mind that he was telling the truth. 'I'll see what I can do. Sheila, come out here luv and look after the bar,' she called. 'I've got business to do. You, come with me,' she said to Ah Fong and taking his arm hustled him down the street to an office marked 'Henry Donaldson, Attorney at Law.'

An hour later, Ah Fong strolled out of Mr Donaldson's Office—the proud owner of a store in Alice Springs.

CHAPTER FORTY-SIX

It was noon and Stella had the day off. Stretching her legs, she lifted her eyes from the book she had borrowed from Dr Bennett and thought about all the things that had happened in the six months since she'd arrived in Alice. She'd settled in at No. 10, begun to study and was working hard either at the hospital or in the Flying Doctor's Office. Needing a break from her studies, she stepped down the three steps to the path in front of the house, crossed the street and walked past a group of aborigines squatting on the corner in the shade of the verandah. She was just about to go into the cafe for a milk shake when her eyes fell on a dark shape huddled behind the aborigines. Blinking, she looked at the strangely familiar shape, the black tunic, the wide trousers. She hesitated, a queasy feeling churned her stomach. 'What do you think Jacko?' she whispered. Jacko ran up and down her arm, his ruff bright green. 'It is her isn't it? Shall I say something?' Instantly Jacko jumped down and ran on fast legs towards the woman.

'Hua?' Stella whispered, leaning towards the huddled form.

Two black eyes looked out from under the hood.

'Hua is it you? Wh . . . what are you doing here?'

'Yes, Stella, it me Hua. Ah Fong come to weigh my Wang's gold. He worry men steal from him if we stay at camp, so we come here. He in there,' she said, nodding in the direction of the lawyer's office.

'I'm so happy to see you Hua,' Stella cried, leaning forward, helping Hua to get up. 'I live over there,' she said, nodding in the direction of the small lodging house. 'Would you like to take tea with me?'

'Tea?' Hua licked her dry lips. 'Yes, Stella, that be nice,' she said and, taking Stella's outstretched hand, hobbled down the street towards No. 10.

CHAPTER FORTY-SEVEN

Billy counted the last cow onto the train and gave a sigh of relief. The Boss would be pleased when he reported that all the cows had got to the collecting yard, that he'd personally counted them on to the trucks. Tucking the receipt into his pocket he made his way to The Royal where he'd booked a room for the night. Tomorrow he'd take a look around Alice before heading back to the Lazy S.

At the bar, he sipped his beer and eyed the two men playing cards in the corner. For a fleeting moment he thought of joining them, but, if he did, Shorty and Jalal would tell the Boss when they got back, so he turned his head away. Over the three day drive from the Lazy S, he'd gained the respect of the two drovers and didn't want to spoil their trust.

'You from the Lazy S?' a voice behind the bar made him jump.

Billy looked up.

Annie was smiling at him.

'Yeah, that's right. The name's Billy. Billy Whitney.'

'Whitney?' Annie's smile faded as she puzzled in her mind, trying to remember where she's heard the name. 'Whitney sounds familiar, but I can't recall . . . never mind . . . my name's Annie by the way and I own this establishment. This your first time in Alice?'

Billy nodded, his eyes straying back to the gamblers.

'You want a game?' Annie asked.

Billy shook his head, took another sip of beer, smiled at Annie and said. 'Yep, I brought the stock down this time. Jake's a bit crook at the moment, and the Boss sent me—wanted to see how I got on,' he grinned. 'It's been a hard day Ma'am, so I think I'll be getting to my room. I'll be going back to the Lazy S as soon as Shorty and Japal get back.'

'That might not be for a while if I know those two,' she laughed, leaning over the bar, looking at him with steely eyes. 'They're good stockmen, but they go walkabout when they're in Alice. So don't be too sure about getting back to the Lazy S tomorrow.'

'We'll see,' he replied over his shoulder, walking towards the stairs. He was half way up when Annie called after him.

'You don't have a sister do you? By the name of Stella?'

The earth slipped from under Billy's feet. 'I might have,' he answered cautiously, heart thumping. 'Why d' you ask?'

'Well, there's a young girl living with Nora at No. 10—spends her days down at the Flying Doctor's office. Says she wants to be a Flying Doctor.'

'Don't sound like my sister,' Billy said. Wallujabi's words rang in his ears, but he'd said she was in Tennant Creek, not Alice. No, it couldn't possibly be Stella.

'She's a pretty thing . . . long blonde hair . . . amber coloured eyes.'

Billy pulled up with a start. 'Amber coloured eyes, you say?'

'Yeah, that's right.'

'Stella living in Alice? No, it must be somebody like her,' he answered, and dismissing the idea that it might be his sister, ran up the stairs to his room.

'You know everything that goes on round here?' Billy asked the pretty woman who brought his breakfast. Shorty was staying at his sister's place. He wasn't sure where Japal was, but one thing he was sure about, they would be there the next morning when it was time to return to the Lazy S. In the meantime, he was free to spend the rest of the day as he wished. Pulling the copy of his father's map out of his pocket, he asked. 'You know where this is?'

'Looks like the aborigine site in the MacDonnell's,' the waitress replied, taking the dirty piece of paper from his hand. 'You're new in town aren't yer. From the Lazy S, I hear?'

Billy nodded. 'Yeah, thought I'd look up a couple of prospector friends. Their name's are Zach Wellsley and Ned Jones and the last time I saw of 'em was out at this place.'

'My name's Sheila, by the way,' the girl replied, placing a large plate of mince and beans in front of him. 'The aborigines reckon this is their Dreaming land and don't like people goin' up there,' she said, handing the paper back to Billy. 'Zach Wellesley, Ned Jones, you say? I don't remember the names, but I did 'ear two men was lost somewhere out there. The Rangers found the bones of one. The other had gone mad—found him out in the desert—barely alive. If they're the men you're looking for, you'd best go and see Jack—Ranger Jack—he patrols the area from Darwin to Alice. If anybody knows, he will. The Police Station's down that way,' she said pointing down the street.

'Thanks,' Billy smiled and walked out into the sunshine.

CHAPTER FORTY-EIGHT

The sun beat off the tin roofs. Billy leaned against the wooden rail running along the side of the verandah and watched the hazy whirls of dust skidding along the street. Taking off his hat, he mopped his forehead. A rustle in the scrub grass growing under the verandah made him look down. 'Oh, it's you Wallujabi. Wondered how long it would be before you showed up again,' he said, staring at the snake's black head. 'What do you want?'

'I give Billy warning,' the snake said.

'Warning. What is it this time?'

'You no go to cave Billy. Your friends Shorty and Japaljarri they Aborigine—cave belong their Spirits—their Dreaming.'

'But . . . what about my pa's gold strike? That's in the cave.'

'You go there Billy, you die. Find sister. She here,' Wallujabi hissed and hearing footsteps echoing further along the verandah, slithered back into the grass.

Billy stared at the spot where the snake had disappeared. Why did it keep coming back to annoy him? The train's whistle drew his attention. It was leaving with the Boss's cows on board. Still feeling pleased with the way the cattle drive had gone, he smiled. But there was nothing wrong with asking at the Police Station if they'd heard anything about his friends, he assured himself. That wouldn't do any harm.

'G'day,' Billy said, stepping into the Police Station, taking off his hat. 'I'm looking for Jack, the Ranger from Darwin.'

'You're looking at him,' replied the man standing beside the desk.

Billy ran his eyes over the tall, tanned man wearing an open neck shirt and shorts.

'And what can I do for you, young man.'

'The names Billy, Billy Whitney, and I . . .

Jack interrupted. 'And you're looking for your sister Stella?'

'Well no. I've heard there's a girl in Alice who's supposed to look like my sister, but I'm looking for two men, Zach Wellsley and Ned Jones. I was told at The Royal you might know something about them, where they might be?'

Jack rubbed his chin, looked thoughtful. After a while he asked, 'And why would a young man like you want to know about two of the most wanted men in the Northern Territory?'

'W . . . wanted men?' Billy stuttered.

'Sure, they're wanted for robbery, swindling and card sharping and a few other things.

'They are?'

'Sure. We identified the bones of one of them. Ned Jones it was. There were bits of his personal belongings outside a cave in the MacDonnell's. The other man we found in the desert. He's in the hospital here. We think it's Zach Wellsley. He was nearly dead from thirst when we found 'im. He's recovering slowly, but the doctors don't think his mind will ever mend. If you know him, perhaps you could give us a positive identification?'

Shaken by what Jack had told him, Billy could only manage to nod in reply. He shivered—Wallujabi's words echoed in his head. 'If you go in cave, you die.'

CHAPTER FORTY-NINE

Stella wandered out of the Flying Doctor's office into the early morning sunshine. She stopped for a moment to watch the colourful lorikeets squabbling noisily over their positions on the wire fence then walked quickly out of Alice to the red boulders where she knew Ah Fong would be doing his kung fu routine.

'Good morning Ah Fong. How are you,' she said, smiling happily when he jumped down beside her. 'How's the store going? Well, I hope.'

'Good morning, Stella. Yes, emporium doing very well. Today more things for store come on train from Darwin,' he said proudly, trying to keep the excitement out of his voice. 'Things for Hua's clinic come also,' he said, giving Stella a questioning look.

'That's good Ah Fong. I've been very busy working at The Flying Doctor's office,' she said, explaining her absence, 'but when I have my next day off I'll come and see Hua. She can show me her new clinic.'

'That good Stella. Mother like that. She miss you,' he said, smiling. 'Maybe you look at emporium too?' he added shyly.

'I'd like that Ah Fong. Maybe we can take tea together,' she said, thinking it might be a good way of getting to know them again. 'The train should be here about 11.00 o'clock. Will you go to meet it?'

'Yes, but there is much to do before that time, so I must go now Stella,' he said, turning to leave.

'OK, see you later then,' she called after him, at the same time admiring the way the early morning sun struck the rock and changed its colour. On her way back to the Flying Doctor's Office, she bumped into the long lean figure of Jack the Ranger.

'Hello Stella. I was hoping to see you.'

'You were? I have to be at the hospital in a few minutes so I can't stay.'

'In that case you don't mind if I walk with you?'

'Of course not. You visiting?'

'Yeah, you might say that. I've arranged to meet someone there and thought I would also take a look at the man in the Observation Ward—we think it's a man called Zach Wellsley,' he said, looking into her face to see her reaction.

'Zach Wellsley? My brother used to hang out with a man by that name. What's he in the hospital for?'

'Oh we found him in the desert, gone mad he had.'

'Was he alone?'

'Was when we found him.'

'I'll have to get someone to take you in, I'm not allowed in that section,' Stella said, pushing the door open.

'Just a minute Stella, there's somebody here I think you might know,' Jack said.

Stella looked over his shoulder, squinted into the darkened foyer. A man stepped forward. 'Stella?'

'Billy!' she cried as her brother stepped out of the shadow. Before she knew what was happening, she had flung herself into his arms.

'Stel? Is it really you?' Billy asked holding her at arm's length.

'Yes, b . . . but . . . how come you're here in Alice?'

'OK you two,' Jack interrupted, a smile curling the corner of his mouth. 'I think you should go and spend a bit of time together. I'll explain everything to Dr Bennett—tell him you won't be in today. In the circumstances I'm sure he'll understand. Billy, before you go, can you spare a minute to identify the patient I told you about?'

'Sure, Jack,' Billy replied. 'Wait here Stel, I won't be long,' he said, following Jack down the corridor to the Observation Ward.

At a door marked 'Patient not known' Jack stopped. 'You ready Billy?'

Billy nodded.

Over Jack's shoulder, Billy stared at the gaunt wild-eyed man muttering strange words.

'Do you know him?' Jack asked.

Billy nodded. 'Yes, it's Zach. But what's happened to him?'

'We don't know Billy. My Rangers found him alone in the desert. The funny thing was he didn't have anything with him—no horse, no tent, nothing. The sun had got to him and he's been daft ever since. The doctors say he's had some sort of shock and they don't think his mind will ever recover. Do you happen to know if he had any relatives?'

'Not that I know of,' Billy replied. 'He only had one real friend and that was Ned. That's all I know about him.'

'We found human bones and some of Ned's clothing outside a cave not far from where we found Zach. We think Ned must have gone into the cave. What happened after that, we don't know. It's Aborigine land up there and who knows what might have happened.'

Billy's stomach turned over.

Seeing his face turn pale, Jack led him from the room and closed the door. 'Thanks Billy,' he said quietly. 'Now I think you'd better go and see your sister. Before you leave Alice call in at the office will you?

There are a couple of forms I'd like you to sign—just to close the books you understand?'

Billy nodded. Strangely, he didn't feel sorry for his friends, just sad. Once more Wallujabi's words rang in his ears. He shivered slightly then smiled when he saw Stella walking towards him.

Stella reached out and took his hand. 'C'mon Billy, I live just down the main street. Let's go down there and talk. I've got so much to tell you,' she said excitedly, pulling him towards the door.

'Yeah, good idea, Stel. I've got a job at a cattle station about 50 miles from here. It's called the Lazy S and I've done really well since I've been there,' he told her proudly. 'The Boss says he's looking for someone to take over Jake's job—he's the senior cattleman. He's not been well lately and the Boss says he's considering me for the job. That's good isn't it Stel?'

Eyes shining, Stella smiled at him. 'Yes, Billy, that's great,' she said, opening the door to the house where she lived.

'So you see why it's important I start back early tomorrow. Can't let the Boss down Stel,' he replied following her inside.

'No you can't do that, but we've got today,' she added, leading him towards the kitchen. 'And now we've found each other, you'll come back won't you?' she asked anxiously.

'Of course, Stel. The cattle drive went well and I'm sure the Boss will let me bring another herd to Alice if I get back to the Lazy S when I'm supposed to. Now tell me how did you come to be working in Alice? I can't wait to hear all your news.'

'OK, but first I'll get Nora to get some tea for us. I'm sure she'd like to meet you.'

Later, when they were sitting on the verandah at the back of the house and Stella had finished telling him her story she said, 'It's good to hear you're doing well Billy. It's hard to believe though we've had to come all the way to Alice Springs to meet up again.'

'Yes, it certainly is strange,' he laughed.

'Dhakhan said it was my .,..'

'What did you say Stel?'

'Nothing,' she laughed, 'I was just agreeing.'

CHAPTER FIFTY

Six months' later, Billy returned to Alice with another herd of cattle and Stella arranged for Jack to take them out to the place where their father had been found.

'That's where we found your pa,' Jack said, pointing to a shady spot near a large boulder.

'This is where I came with Zach and Ned,' Billy whispered to Stella.

'You sure Billy?'

'Yes, Stella, I'm quite sure. If you look between those layers of rock you can just see the cave's entrance,' he said, pointing in the direction of the dark area.

Jack drew his horse alongside Stella's. 'I'll leave you to say your farewells,' he muttered shyly. 'But don't be long, there's a storm brewing. They can be very fierce out here. I'll be back in fifteen minutes. OK?'

Stella nodded. Slowly she dismounted, walked over to the boulder and sank down beside it. Tears tumbled. 'It must have been hard for pa, dying out here on his own.'

Billy nodded, but he wasn't listening. He was staring at the cave's dark entrance.

'We can't go in there, Billy,' Stella said sharply, seeing the hunger in her brother's eyes. 'We've got to forget pa's gold strike. You know what Wallujabi said—those who go into the cave will die and now you know what happened to Zach and Ned you believe it, don't you? Let's say our good-byes to pa and leave. We've both got new lives—futures to look forward to—and we don't really know if the gold's in there anyway.'

Billy looked at his sister and shook his head. 'No we don't,' he admitted finally as the first drops of rain splattered on his hands.

'Come on then, let's say good-bye to pa.'

Standing in the rain, heads bowed, they said their own good-byes. Stella took the worn piece of paper from her pocket, tore it into shreds and tossed it into the air. The wind snatched at the pieces, spreading them in all directions. 'Good-bye pa,' she said, her tears joining the rain. 'You weren't to know this was Aborigine Dreaming land and if you did find gold here, then it wasn't yours to take. Rest in peace,' she whispered.

Billy watched Stella toss the map into the wind. 'Good-bye pa. I'll never forget what you tried to do for us,' he whispered.

Thunder rumbled in the distance.

Slowly they began to walk back to where Jack waited with the horses. Suddenly Wallujabi's long black body sped towards them.

'Wallujabi,' Billy muttered.

'Yes Billy, Wallujabi is glad you and Stella leave now. This place belong to my ancestor. It Dreaming place and sacred for Aborigines.'

'Yes, Wallujabi,' Billy replied wearily. 'We've only come to say good-bye to our pa.'

Wallujabi waved his head to and fro. 'Good-bye Billy,' he hissed. Suddenly his body began to change—the shape of a human appeared—Dhakhan was standing in front of them, rain running down his gleaming body.

'Dhakhan! You're not?' Stella cried.

Dhakhan smiled and nodded. 'Yes, Stella of the Skies. I am also Wallujabi—protector of the Aborigines and their laws. But I am also your friend and I will come if you call my name three times.'

'Thank you Dhakhan, I'll remember,' she replied, taking Billy's hand. 'Have we reached out destiny Dhakhan?'

Dhakhan nodded his head, but he was already beginning to fade. 'Do not forget Stella of the Skies . . . call if you need me.' Then he was gone.

'This is the real Australia Billy,' Stella said, waving her arms in the direction of the red rocks where Dhakhan had disappeared. 'We must make our lives here and help the Aborigines keep their Dreaming sites for their children's children. That is our destiny.'

'Yes, Stel,' Billy agreed. 'This is the land of the Aborigine and they are right to want to protect it.'

Hand in hand, they walked back to where Jack waited. As they rode away, Stella looked over her shoulder at the cave's entrance. Was the gold really there, she wondered? Now, they would never know, but perhaps the Aborigines didn't want the white man to know.

©

Author Biography

Nancy Lou Deane has travelled widely, living in Australia, UK and Trinidad. Writing adventure stories for children began when she lived on Dartmoor in Devon UK, (England's last southern wilderness) and became fascinated by the moor's legendary ghosts and spooks. Currently she is living in Hampshire in UK and writing every day is the life she now enjoys.

Her third book, Gold Fever, is set in Australia and continues her theme of spirits and strange happenings. Her other books are: Terror at Ullick Farm and Island of Spirits. Those who have asked to know more about Percy (in Terror at Ullick Farm) will be interested to read Meg's Secret –out soon.

Nancy Lou Deane can be contacted via her website:
www.nancyloudeane.com

Lightning Source UK Ltd.
Milton Keynes UK
177072UK00005B/7/P